Ronny's Songs

A Novel

Tom Brooks

New Friends Publishing, LLC

Ronny's Songs

ISBN-13: 978-1-940354-01-9

Ronny's Songs is based in part on the true life story of
the author, who has tried to recreate events,
locales, and conversations from his memories.
In order to maintain their anonymity, in some instances,
he has changed the names of some individuals
and some identifying characteristics.

Cover Design by
Anne Cote and Layne Walker
All rights reserved

Cover Picture by
Tom Brooks
All rights reserved

Published by
New Friends Publishing, LLC
Lake Havasu City, AZ

Printing history
First edition published in August 2013

Dedication

To my Dad,
for his unknowing willingness to play the sometimes,
somewhat, embellished role as the antagonistic character.

Acknowledgments

I have to thank my wife Pamela for reading *Ronny's Songs* back to me a hundred times. I look back over the past five years and can only hope I would have done the same for her. Thanks to Gladys Engstrom for telling me more than once to put the stories of my life on paper. Thanks to Mitch Ma for teaching me the great things a computer can do for a writer. Thanks for patient, smart men like my editor William Greenleaf and my publisher Layne Walker. Thanks to Mom, Dad, and my brothers and sisters for the greatest learning experiences of my life.

Table of Contents

Chapter 1
Mildred and Herman Were Lovers

"Hey, Tommy," my mother yelled from the top of the basement stairs. She was wearing one of her two faded pastel housedresses under a multi-stained floral apron. During most of the day she kept her hair in spit curls pressed to her scalp with bobby pins. On hot days or when she was tired, she wore her hose rolled down to mid-calf. Mom's friends said that she cleaned up really nice. She was five foot five and had blue eyes and what she said was a little baby fat around her middle. I didn't know how, but Dad got blamed for that. Before he arrived home, she always pulled out the bobby pins and ran a brush through her hair, and the curls popped up.

This sweet, uneducated, yet intuitive lady also had a black-and-white Sunday dress. She accented this forties-style vintage dress with a cheap-looking hat, pinned with a flowered ornament of sorts. She wore this same outfit to church and on rare special occasions. She would stand there rubbing her nervous little hands together and ask, "How do I look, Tommy? Will your daddy think I look nice?"

I wish that I had told her just once that she looked beautiful. As a not-so-bright nine-year-old with a limited vocabulary, I usually replied with an unknowingly uncomplimentary response. "You look okay."

"Do you and your brother want to ride in the police car? Your father has to go back into the city to check on one of his stool pigeons."

I had been climbing and sliding down the high coal piles at the Oakley coal yard off Paxton Avenue. The coal yard was off-limits. The obvious reason was all over me. My ingenious way back into the basement by sliding down the coal shoot into the cellar didn't help my situation. I worked the scrub brush and washboard as fast as I could.

Stool pigeon. I had never heard of that type of pigeon. I wondered if they were different from the pigeons walking around down at People's Corner. I had given up trying to catch one of those years ago.

I rinsed off my shirt and pants and mixed them in with some other dirty clothes in the wringer washer. I was glad Mom didn't come down the stairs and see me covered with black soot. She would have sprayed me off with the cold hose. I started weaving my way through the sheets and towels hanging in the basement on rigged-up clotheslines nailed into the cement walls. My mom used these lines when it was cold or wet outside. The only light bulb hung over the washtubs, now twenty feet behind me, and it was out. The basement was dark, with the familiar smell of damp, musty clothes and the burning of coal. I sidestepped through the last line of defense, barely touching the laundry.

Barely was appropriate, because I was bare naked, holding one of my coal-covered Buster Brown shoes in each hand. At least now I could see a shadowed outline of the stair railing. It was down and to my right, where the light crept under the door at the top. Down and to my left was the furnace with its door cracked open. As I went to close the door, a stilled image appeared.

"Holy crap!" I screamed.

The burning coals threw an orange glow across a big-eared, freckle-faced, redheaded Ronny, who was smiling. Ronny was one of my brothers.

"You scared the heck out of me," I said.

He stopped smiling and looked down at my feet.

"What's wrong with you?" I yelled.

There was a big rat a few inches from my foot, with an eight-inch rope for a tail. The steel spring bar of the wooden trap lay across its back instead of its neck. Ronny had slid off the floor cover to the rat-infested sewer drain. He sat Indian style on top of an orange crate, with pen and paper in hand, watching and waiting for the kill.

"Why didn't you say something?" I asked. "Were you going to let me step on that rat?"

"Yep," he said, as his smile slowly reappeared.

"Boys," Mom yelled down with a bit of sarcasm in her

voice, "if your father, the great Cincinnati detective Jim Brooks, honks his horn, that means don't bother. He's already gone."

"We're coming!" I yelled. "Come on, Ronny, close the furnace door and let's go."

He picked up the rat by the tail. It was still half alive, mouth opened, with a full set of teeth. The trap was clamped firmly into its back. Ronny started wiggling the rodent in front of my face, then underhanded it toward my privates, which by then were blocked by my left shoe. I hit the trap with the heel of my right shoe, knocking it out of his hand. Still in the trap, the rat began slowly crawling away, pulling the trap and its body with its two front legs. Ronny stepped on the rat, grabbed its tail, tossed the suffering rodent into the fire, and closed the door. He picked up his pen and paper from off the crate, put them in his back pocket, and started up the stairs.

"Hey, is that a drawing?" I asked. "Am I allowed to tell Dad about your pictures, just not your writings? I thought you only wrote . . ."

He stopped halfway up, spun around, flew down the steps, and grabbed me by the back of the neck. He opened the furnace door and shoved my face close to the opening. "Do you feel the heat?" he whispered in my ear as he continued to squeeze.

What kind of question was that, with my hair starting to singe right before he released his vice grip?

"Tommy, need I remind you of our little secret and its associated penalty? Wasn't the torturous death of the rat enough? Do I need to remind you of what will happen to you?"

"You don't scare me," I lied.

"For your sake, I hope I do." He thumped up the wooden stairs and out the door.

I'd heard Mom tell Dad more than once that she sometimes worried about Ronny's dark side. The only reason I thought I knew what she meant was because of her Bible stories. In them God was always the light, and the devil was always dark. I had asked my older brother Jimmy why Mom thought one of Ronny's sides was dark. He said she started saying that back when Ronny was very young. He was playing with matches, which was bad enough in the first place. The fact that he was burning the legs off grasshoppers and watching them die was a whole other thing. I could only imagine the spanking he must have gotten. I could only imagine because no one would tell me.

Anyway, understanding why became much more intriguing to me then telling. Ronny would write in plain sight, but I was never allowed to bring attention to it. At the time, I had no idea how clever he was with words for his age. Apparently no one else did either. I did notice that he talked more grown-up, using big words, when I was the only one around.

There were six kids in the house: four boys and two girls, as well as Mildred the dog—that is, when she was allowed in the house. She did get to spend a few days of every year in the basement. Mom would say, "Mildred's in heat and getting hotter." Then she would laugh to herself. When Millie was heated, it wouldn't be long before Herman would be over, sniffing around.

Herman was a big black-and-white dog from two houses down. I didn't know how he ever found the house, since his long hair covered his eyes. Mom told me he could smell his way. They said he was a sheepdog, but I'm sure he'd never seen a sheep. Mildred was a small-to-medium size dog with short, brown, shaggy hair. She even tried to sneak out of the basement door to get to Herman. When I asked Mom why, she said it was because Mildred and Herman were lovers and wanted to make puppies. We couldn't allow that to happen because Dad wouldn't let them live.

Ronny was already upstairs, and I was still naked, hoping not to hear the car horn. Lucky for me our clothes hamper was actually the bottom landing of the stairs. If we didn't throw our clothes down there, they didn't get washed. I kicked on a somewhat dirty pair of pants that I had thrown down three days ago. The flannel lining had a few rips and tears that had redesigned its red-and-black plaid.

I grabbed a large, somewhat smelly T-shirt off the floor. It was a toss-up as to whose armpits were in it last: Jimmy's, Bobby's, or Ronny's. Yes, I'm sure it was very time-consuming for my parents when they had to pick the next boy's name. Sister Norma was the next oldest after Jimmy, and Nancy was the youngest, six years behind me. They were off-limits.

"Never try to have fun at their expense," Dad said. "Don't tease, don't touch."

Even Ronny followed Dad's orders.

I ran through the house, out the front door, and took two jumps down the stoop. Ronny was in the backseat with the doors locked. He was holding his rat drawing up against the window. I had to admit, it looked pretty real with only the streetlight shining.

"It's cold out here!" I yelled. "Open the door."

Ronny just smiled. Dad, who was across the yard talking with my uncle, echoed my request. Ronny obeyed, but he took his sweet time.

"Move over and let me in." I shivered and stuck my palms together between my thighs.

"Dad only said for me to open the door."

Okay, that was enough. Now I was mad. I had both Buster Browns dug into the ground. "Geronimo!" I screamed.

I threw a right forearm into his ribs and a left across the side of his neck. I bit my folded tongue between my front teeth for extra power and pushed with all my might. Ronny was not moving. He wouldn't unless he wanted to or Dad made him. All the neighbors said Ronny was a big boy for barely turning thirteen. I was short and skinny but still hoped that in four more years I would be that big too. I felt okay about being small—I mean, looking from the inside out. Oh well, that was me. When Ronny was my age, no one had called him a runt like they did me. Even if he had been a runt, I would have advised against calling him any names.

Uncle Lou had stopped by to talk about the Boy Scouts' paper drive coming up that next weekend. He had big muscles and was six foot tall. That was three of my fingers taller than Dad. He always wore dress pants and a white T-shirt with no sleeves. He was really my dad's first cousin. For some odd reason, if relatives were as old as my parents, it showed respect to call them aunt or uncle. I wondered why we just didn't call him First Cousin Lou.

Dad used Uncle Lou's truck to take the Scouts around to people's houses asking for old newspapers. The Scouts sold them by the pound to a middleman, who cleaned the ink off the paper in some magic way. Then he made money selling it back to the guy who printed on it again. At least, that's how Ronny explained it to me.

Dad wouldn't let Ronny go with the Scouts anymore because he had pushed me off the truck. I was too young to be a Scout, but Dad let me ride in the back of the truck with them when they went to return it to Uncle Lou. Ronny dared me to jump off the truck before it came to a complete stop at a light, then jump back on right when the light turned green again. I had to jump before we stopped at my uncle's, or I was a chicken. Believe me, I wanted to jump because I thought it would be fun. Plus, it would show those older guys that I wasn't scared.

"I double dare you!" Ronny cried as we turned off Duck Creek Road.

Now I had to jump.

Dad put the truck into low gear as we entered the driveway. The plan was to jump four feet out from six foot up, onto the front lawn. I placed my left hand on top of the cab, my right leg over the side, heel back in between the truck's wooden slates for push off. I slung my left leg over high and hard toward the green carpet of grass. I was hoping for a perfect tuck-and-roll landing.

Unexpectedly, Ronny gave me a push. The heel of my right shoe got hung up between the two boards. I fell straight down onto the cement, flat on my stomach. With the air knocked out of me, I rolled around with my legs still under the moving truck. The Scouts yelled for me to pull my legs out, but the fact that I couldn't breathe was first on my mind.

Luckily, Dad had to double clutch in order to get up the sloped driveway. This gave me time to get my left leg out, but the back wheel ran over the lower part of my right leg. It blew up like a baseball and was black and blue for weeks. My leg looked like one of the sausages hanging in Johnny's Delicatessen. Everyone said they couldn't believe that I didn't break something. The doctor said a nerve was crushed and that maybe it would grow back. If not, the muscle would be smaller than the left one.

Talk about getting crushed. Dad beat Ronny really bad that day. Dad started in on Ronny with openhanded slaps to the head, calling him stupid with every swing. Then he threw a couple of hard-fisted punches to the stomach and kicked him in the rear end a few times. He took off his belt, doubled it over, and began whipping him on the back.

I was crying, asking my dad to please stop.

Finally, Uncle Lou stopped holding me, got up, grabbed Dad's arm, and said firmly, "That's enough, Jim!"

For weeks afterward, when I thought of Ronny on that day, it made me weak down in my stomach, and my chest burned. On replaying my failed Superman jump in my head, I realized that Ronny was lifting and pushing. Maybe he was trying to make sure that I made it to the grass. Before I could even finish asking him why he didn't explain it to Dad, he interrupted me.

"It wouldn't have done any good, Tommy; it's just the way it is."

"Sometimes my heart still feels heavy from the tears Dad made me cry that day," I said.

Ronny pulled out his pen and paper and told me to move on. "Thank you, Tommy," he said faintly as I walked away.

That surprised me. *Thank you* and *please* weren't used between us brothers and sisters unless Mom forced us.

~~~

Whenever I saw Dad mad, Ronny was usually on the receiving end. A couple years back, when we lived over in Evanston, Dad was still a uniform patrolman. A police call went into Precinct Seven that a young boy was stealing reflectors off license plates at a local car lot. My dad just happened to take the call. When he walked into the auto dealership, the salesman pointed toward the chairs in the waiting area.

Ronny's face wore a discouraged, you've-got-to-be-kidding-me look. I could read his mind as if it were typed on that cleaned, reused newspaper. It read, *Of all the cops in this town, he gets the call.*
~~~

Dad simply said, "I'll take care of this, young man."

The fat salesman sat down, smirked, and interlocked his fingers behind his big bald head. Then he leaned back in his rolling chair and swirled his feet up on top of the desk. His foot-long tie with the double-knot Windsor jumped up against his chin.

"Stand up, turn around, and put your hands behind your back," Dad ordered.

Ronny stood up with rounded shoulders, head forward, and eyes to the floor.

My being short had paid off for me that night. I was two cars down and two rows up. Ronny got nabbed right when I was about to blurt out that I had found two bright red quarter-size reflectors. For a dime they were going to look good on somebody's bicycle fender. I ducked under a car and looked down the row. All I could see was Ronny's motorcycle boots, a foot off the ground, headed in the wrong direction. That salesman with the big head and even bigger belly put Ronny in a full nelson. He carried him into the building, slammed him down in a chair, and told him to stay put. I motioned through the display window for him to run out. He had a couple of good chances while old melon head was using the phone, but he just kept giving me the go-away sign.

When Dad pushed him out through the car dealer's double doors, Ronny fell, breaking the corner bricks off a planter. He rubbed his leg through his ripped pants, just below his right front Levi pocket. I could tell Ronny was crying on the inside. The sad, hurt look on his face gave him away. From his knees, he spotted me hiding behind the front fender of a candy-apple red Ford. My mouth was pressed against the bumper, and I was looking at him cross-eyed. He couldn't help but smile.

Dad grabbed a handful of Ronny's thick, straight red hair and yanked him to his feet. "You think this is funny? I'll give you something to smile about when we get to the house!"

He gripped the cuffs between Ronny's wrists and raised his arms up high behind his back. This made Ronny bend forward at the hips. He kept telling Dad that it was hurting his shoulders, really bad. Dad backhanded him a couple of times and shoved him headfirst into the backseat of the patrol car.

"How dumb do you have to be to do something that stupid?" Dad yelled.

I wanted to ask Dad what the answer was to that question. I mean, just how dumb is stupid? Was there a measurement for small, medium, or large? How was Ronny supposed to answer? Maybe it was one of those sayings that grown-ups used that didn't make sense.

The house was only five blocks away. If Dad drove the speed limit, I could beat them home. I took off cutting through the back yards, down a couple of alleys, jumping a few small fences, and praying that the Olivers' dog, Blackie, was inside. Old Blackie never barked, and at night it was hard to see him. You never knew when or if he was going to sneak up and bite you in the behind. When we played Kick the Can, little Ralph Oliver had to make sure that "Butt-biter Blackie" was in the house. Mom liked to warn us, but couldn't do so without laughing. "If you're going past the Olivers', keep one hand on your zuzu and the other on your derriere. Old Blackie might be hungry." Life wasn't easy for Mom, but she could still make herself laugh and laugh at herself.

I made it through the front door; Blackie was at the bottom of the stoop with his tongue hanging out.

"I got you, dog. I'm just too fast."

He started walking away and looked back at me as if to say, *Next time*.

The drill had already started, and all of us boys had been through it more than once. Of course, Ronny was in first place. Dad had just made him go upstairs, strip down to his underwear, and get into bed. Dad was outside the door, taking off his three-inch-wide police belt, nice and slow. From inside the bedroom you could hear the big ring of keys jiggling. They hung from a hook on the belt next to the row of bullets. Sometimes he took the keys off and folded the belt over. I never figured out which way was worse. It seemed like he swung harder with the belt doubled over. Bobby and I had learned that the sooner you yelled and cried, the sooner he stopped, but not Ronny.

It wasn't like someone got a beating daily or even weekly. The last time was almost two months before. Ronny and I were down at the Ritz movie theater. We had already sat through this movie once, and I was getting a little bored. The neighbors said Mom used this place like it was a babysitter.

When we wanted to go to a picture show, she would do her best to find us the money. She would go through Dad's coat pockets, looking for loose change. We even checked under the pillows of the couch. If she couldn't scrape up enough, she would tell us to cash in the pop bottles and "get out of my hair."

When I'd ask her if she wanted to come, she always had an excuse—like, "No thanks, I have a clothesline full of laundry that should be taken down." I remember that excuse. Ronny had to take time to write something in his homemade pad of loose writing paper. We missed the first part of the Road Runner cartoon because of him. I didn't mind missing the newsreel, but I did mind missing the cartoon. I didn't understand why Mom would tell us to get out of her hair instead of her house.

On the way to the delicatessen to get our two-cents-per-bottle deposit money, Ronny tried to explain. "Tommy, it's just a saying."

"Yes," I responded, "I know Mom is saying it, but who else is saying it, and why are they saying it?"

Ronny gave me an exasperated look. "Now listen. You know Johnny at the deli?"

"You know I know Johnny!"

"Okay, remember last Saturday, when you bought the two pieces of Mary Jane candy with your penny, and you asked him if he wanted one?"

"Yeah, I remember."

"And what did he say?"

"He said, 'No thanks, I just had my shoes shined.'"

"There you go. That's just a saying."

"But his shoes—"

Ronny put his hand over my mouth. "If you tell me that

his shoes were dirty, I'll knock you into next week."

"Next week?"

Ronny balled up his fist, and I quickly told him, "I know, that's just another saying."

With a single knuckle to my head, he replied, "No, that's not just a saying. I mean it; you won't wake up till the second Tuesday of next week!"

"Second Tuesday . . . ?" I was really confused.

Ronny told me not to, but I started throwing ice and juju beads up into the balcony. That was a real smart move. We were sitting only two rows out from the edge of the balcony. I had to throw up; they got to throw down. They could see me; I couldn't see them. I sure couldn't spit that high up, but they could sure spit down. However, their aim wasn't "right on the money."

That was another one of those sayings. The baseball announcer on the radio a few days before had said, "The throw all the way from Wally Post to Ted Kluszewski was right on the money."

No, it was "right on the bag."

There was a big yellow wad of spit "right on Ronny's cheek" that I was sure was meant for me. His eyelids started pinching together, and the veins in his neck were popping out. Ronny could get mad really quick but then let it go or hold it in. I didn't know which or when. Bobby said he lived between anger and fear. When I asked him what that meant, he said it meant he was crazy. Bobby was the crazy one if he thought Ronny was afraid of anyone, except maybe Dad.

I had my shirt in my mouth and slid down in my seat trying to keep from laughing. Ronny wiped the spit onto my sleeve, slugged me in the arm, and told me to stay seated. He got up and moved down about five rows.

The usher had already shined the flashlight on me twice that day. One more time and I would have been kicked out. On the way down the aisle, Ronny popped a handful of what I thought were juju beads into his mouth. At least seven more minutes of the *Seven Year Itch* had played. I was hoping he would be ready to go home—that is, after he got to see the dress blow up on that pretty lady again.

I couldn't see Ronny's head anymore. What I could see

were the heads of the people hanging over the balcony. They were looking my way and cursing, saying they were going to kill the cat with the peashooter, that he won't think he's so cool when they jam that peashooter down his damn throat. So it wasn't candy Ronny had put in his mouth. The usher headed back up the aisle to see what was going on in the balcony. Some outside light flashed into the theater from the far-left front-side exit door.

Okay, it was time for me to leave. I ran up the aisle and pushed open the lobby doors to freedom. Instead I had two men pointing their fingers at me.

"Right here, young man. Don't you move!" It was the head usher, the older man who wore the bell captain type uniform. "You're one of the Brooks boys from across Montgomery, on the other side of the cemetery, aren't you?"

"Yeah."

"You say 'yes, sir' when you talk to me. You understand me?"

"Yes, sir."

"Give me the peashooter."

"I don't have a peashooter."

"You're telling me it wasn't you who sprayed the people in the balcony, almost putting someone's eye out?"

"No."

"No, what?"

"No, sir, but I did toss some candy up there."

I got a little scared then, because I didn't want to tell on Ronny. The usher started in on me again.

"Was that your brother with you today?"

"Yes . . . yes, sir."

"Where is he?"

"He left a long time ago."

"Was he the one with the peashooter?"

"I never saw it."

"You're telling me you did not see him pea-shooting in the theater?"

"Yeah, I never saw him. That's the truth."

"I know your folks. You tell them you are not allowed back in the theater until they talk with me."

"You know my dad is a policeman?"

"I don't care what he is. You give that punk brother of yours a message. If I find out that he was the shooter, it'll be a cold day in he knows where before he's allowed back in here!"

Wow, even the usher was saying sayings.

Mom didn't want me to lie. She said to "always tell the truth; one lie just leads to another."

I didn't lie answering the questions, but I knew it was Ronny. God knew that I knew it was Ronny, because Mom said God knows everything. I wanted to know if Ronny really knew where it had to be cold before he could get back in the theater.

Mildred And Herman Were Lovers

Mildred and Herman were lovers
Mildred had short scraggly hair
Herman was just another boy on the block
You'd think he was kind of a square

Mildred and Herman had been together for years
But little did Herman know
That every time he would fall asleep
Out the door old Mildred would go

She'd fluff up her hair and hound every bar
To the back doors she would go
She'd walk the streets beneath the city lights
We all knew what she was looking for

Early one morning old Herman awoke
And Mildred he couldn't find
Off in the alley were two hound dogs
With old Mildred just a flashing her eyes

Old Herman a sheepdog he barely could see
Walked up to Mildred and company
Gave a gentle bark that seemed to say
I love ya, I forgive ya, come home with me

Well, Mildred walked with her tail between her legs
In the doghouse I'm sure she'd be
But rumor's around she's top dog in town
With old Herman takin' care of her needs

The moral of the story is plain to me
Check my lady it's Mildred I see
I just hope and pray there's
A whole lot of Herman in me

Chapter 2
Directly From You

Mom said that years ago when I was a baby, Dad never got to come home during working hours. He was a "flatfoot," walking the beat in downtown Cincinnati. Mom said the army didn't even want him because he had flat feet. That saying made sense. If someone walked too much, they got flat feet.

Well, Dad made it home early that pea-shooting night. He walked into the house and went straight to the living room. Ronny was sitting over on the couch using the coffee table to write on.

"Stand up and empty those pockets," Dad ordered.

Dad stood in full uniform, legs apart, looking down at the top of Ronny's head. His right hand rested on the gun handle that stuck out from his hip. His other hand gripped his nightstick that ran down the side of his left thigh.

Ronny didn't bother getting up or reaching into his pockets. He opened the coffee-table drawer and pulled out the peashooter and a fist full of beans. He knew what Dad wanted. Dad pulled out his leather blackjack from the back of his belt and slapped Ronny's paper off the table.

"Hey, those are Ronny's private papers. You don't even know what—" I caught myself, because I could feel the look of cold eyes.

Dad pulled out his nightstick and pointed it toward Ronny. "Go up and get in bed. I'll be up there soon."

"Be careful what you say," Ronny whispered as he strolled on past me.

Dad adjusted his white-and-black police hat with his thumb and index finger. Then he turned toward me. He had pulled his hat down a little too far on his forehead. I could barely see his eyes.

"I hear you like to throw candy at people. Get upstairs.

I'll deal with you, too, when I'm finished talking with your mother."

I didn't know how Dad found things out so fast. He knew everything that was going on in town. He even found out things that happened on the other side of the Ohio River.

It was about eight o'clock at night, and Bobby was already in bed asleep. He had a job setting pins down at the bowling alley on the weekends. Sometimes I got to go down and roll the balls back for him. With his long, lanky legs, he could rack two alleys at a time. He was pushing sixteen and good in school because he could read.

Ronny and I got undressed and into bed.

"Tommy, I'll only give you this information once, so listen closely." He talked softly so as not to wake Bobby. "In the brain there's only a very thin line that separates love and hate. The revealing of my writings to Dad will make my mind cross that line."

"Where did you hear that? Love and hate aren't that close. Love and hate are more like a thermometer."

"Just remember—I get rid of things I hate."

"Don't you want to hear about the thermometer?"

"Not really."

"We have to stay awake and wait for Dad anyway. So, we've been learning about the thermometer in school. We have a big white-and-red one under the clock above the blackboard. It only goes up to a hundred. Water boils at two hundred and twelve degrees and freezes at thirty-two degrees. The mercury falls and rises with the weather. Another name for mercury is liquid silver."

"That's pretty good that you learned that. Are you going to have a test on it?"

"I already failed it. There were only two questions, and I had to get both right to get an *A*. I got the other name for mercury right on the first question. I got all the numbers right. But I forgot to put the *Fs* after the little circle degree sign. I got a big red *F*."

"Well, *F* that, and tell me, what does this have to do with love and hate?"

"I don't know anything about that brain love line. But

when I think of Mom, she'd be at the top of the thermometer. I can't think of anyone that I hate, but if I did, they would be way down past freezing. Nowhere close to boiling like you and Mom."

We all three slept in a double bed. That's the way we started out each night. Usually, one of us gave up and ended up on the floor. It was getting more crowded as we got older and bigger. They made me sleep in the middle with my head down toward the foot of the bed. I could never figure out what their feet smelled like. I just knew it was bad.

My answer came one Sunday while watching Mom make a salad. She opened a bottle, and there was the smell that I went to sleep with every night.

"Mom, what's that?"

"It's vinegar."

"That's what their feet smell like!"

"Whose feet smell like?"

Then she started laughing, laughing so hard that she started crying at the same time. When I said I wasn't kidding, she laughed even harder. She called my aunt to tell her, but she started crying tears, laughing, and couldn't catch her breath. She told her she'd have to call her back. She sat down in the chair, bursting out with laughter every few seconds.

I told her it wasn't funny, that sometimes it took my breath away, it was so strong.

She started holding her stomach, gasping for air.

"Mom, I bet you couldn't make it through one night. I've done it night after night for a long time."

"You poor baby, come here." She started to hug me and then bent over laughing. She ran toward the bathroom holding herself. "I got a hurry call, I got a hurry call," she said, which meant she had to pee. "Oh Jesus, Mary, and Joseph," she yelled.

I guess she didn't make it.

On the night of the pea-shooting incident, we pulled the covers up over our heads and waited, no skin showing except for Bobby's skinny feet sticking out. We stayed still and quiet, hoping Mom could talk Dad out of giving us a beating.

If she couldn't, she would at least beg him not to hit us too hard. After he would leave, she would come up and wrap us in cold, wet dish towels. She even cried with us most of the time. Ronny would get the heck beat out of him and still tell Mom that it was nothing. Not me or Bobby. When Dad hurt us, we wanted her to know and to take care of our wounds.

If Dad wanted to tell us what we did wrong, he would pull the covers off and get us one at a time. He would preach to us about right and wrong. If not, he would just come in swinging the belt. He always made us wait, and ten minutes seemed like forever. During that time, I used to try to figure out what deserved what. Should the punishment for not flushing the toilet be the same as fighting or throwing rocks? I didn't think so. Dad only gave people tickets for running a stop sign. But he put them in jail for driving drunk. There was a difference. It just didn't seem fair sometimes.

I asked Ronny why he got hit more times for cussing the day before than Bobby got hit for talking back to Mom. Talking back to Mom was a real no-no. Ronny told me that sometimes our whippings might not have anything to do with what we did. It might be for what Dad did or didn't do. That made no sense to me. When Dad came in, I was planning on asking him if the beating was for us or for him. If he said him, I was going to ask him for the belt.

He finally walked in with the belt swinging, keys and all. There was no time for questions. The first swing hit Bobby in the ankle by accident, which woke him up screaming. That night Bobby had no clue what was going on. Ronny was smiling, and I started laughing, which of course was the wrong thing to do. Bobby hopped around the room holding his left ankle. He bumped into the cabinet of the old self-standing Zenith radio. The family Bible fell off its top to the floor with a slam. Dad hit us a few more times, then walked out.

Ronny had taken most of the blows. I always tried to stay under him or Bobby as much as possible. It was hard to do when we were all trying to dodge the belt. There weren't a lot of red marks on me that night. The one that made me cry was the one across my ribs. It burned for a long time.

He wouldn't admit it, but Ronny was blocking for me that night. He painfully bent over, picked up the Bible, and put it back on top of the radio. "Bobby, go get Dad to come back and read us a few scriptures," he said facetiously.

"Shut up, stupid," Bobby replied.

That was stupid. Dad never had time to read us scriptures. Mom told the best stories anyway. She told us lots of Bible stories, some more than once. Bobby said she added things or changed them a little to make them more interesting.

"What did you two clowns do now?" Bobby yelled. "Never mind, I don't want to hear it. Oh, my ankle is killing me. Ronny, when are you ever going to grow up? Doggone it, that hurts." He sat on the edge of the bed holding his foot. He rocked back and forth, staring at his ankle. "The outline of the key is on my ankle."

I just had to ask. "Is it the skeleton key? Can I see it?"

"Yeah, if you can still see after I blacken both of your eyes. Now, both of you get out of this bed before I kick you out. You're not sleeping in this bed tonight."

Ronny threw his pillow down, spread out his quilt, and melted onto the floor. He wasn't feeling good, but I wasn't giving up that easy. My leg and side were stinging.

"Hey, this isn't just your bed," I said.

"It is tonight," Bobby answered.

"How can you kick me out of bed? I thought your ankle hurt sooo bad."

"Get out, you little runt, or I'll beat you like you're a one-legged man in an ass-kicking contest."

Just then, I swear I heard Ronny smiling from across the room.

"Tommy, go find a blanket and come over here on the floor," Ronny said.

"Bobby, give me my pillow!"

"Not tonight. It's going to be busy propping up my foot."

"I can't sleep on the floor without a pillow."

"You should have thought of that before you made Dad hit me on the ankle."

"I didn't make Dad hit you!"

"Yes, you did. It's because of you and your crazy brother

over there.”

“He’s not crazy. He’s as smart as you, but just in different ways. Bobby thinks he’s the big Daddy-O, doesn’t he, Ronny?”

“Shut your mouth, shorty,” Bobby said. “Ronny, I need to hear it directly from you. Are you ever going to shape up? One day you say you are, the next day you don’t. After getting in trouble today, you should, but you probably won’t.”

“Tommy, come over here and lie down,” Ronny said. “You can share my pillow tonight.” He put his pad on the floor and started writing.

“So, indirectly that’s a no, because you’re not answering,” Bobby said.

I laid my head on the end of the pillow. The only thing between us and the hardwood floor was a worn-out quilt that used to belong to my mom’s mom.

“Ronny, when Mom says, ‘This quilt has memories,’ she doesn’t really think that quilts can remem—”

“Tommy, it’s just a saying. Now go to sleep.”

“Just one more question. Are those kicking contests on radio or television?”

“On television at midnight. Now go to sleep.”

“I know better than that. Nothing comes on TV after ‘The Star-Spangled Banner,’ except the channel wheel thing.”

“Tommy, be quiet,” Ronny begged nasally.

I lay there for a few minutes thinking about Dad and listening to Bobby’s breathing getting louder. My pillow must have really helped, because that sore ankle sure didn’t keep him from sleeping. “Ronny, do you think Dad loves us?” Just in case Ronny was asleep too, I whispered.

Ronny whispered back, “Dad loves you a whole lot, Tommy.”

“Well, if he loves me, then he loves you.”

“Oh, I don’t know about that.”

“Why don’t you know about that? He can’t love one and not the other.”

“Tommy, this world is made up of people loving one and not the other.” There was a little shaking in Ronny’s voice when he said that last part.

"Well, I love you, Ronny."

His red face was in the pillow, and I was looking at the back of his red head. He didn't say anything to me, but I knew it made him smile, because smiling made his ears move.

Bobby told me that Ronny hadn't laughed out loud since he was a little boy. He said it was because Dad had told him he had an ugly laugh. So, from then on when something was funny to him, he merely smiled. If it was really funny, he smiled big and made a slight gulping sound, trying to swallow his laughter. That's why I'd say, "I could hear Ronny smiling."

Most people wouldn't catch the shaking because his voice was so different anyway. Some said Ronny talked like he had half of a harelip. He had no hair on his lip, so I had no idea what harelip meant. I didn't know what a whole harelip sounded like, much less a half. It was just Ronny. Most of the time, he talked with his tongue down behind the bottom row of his teeth. Sometimes half of his voice would come out of his nose.

When I could catch Mom at the right time, she gave me answers to my questions. If I asked too many, she ran me off.

"You put her into overwhelm with all your dumb questions," my older sister, Norma, told me. I wondered if she meant overdrive.

Dad said that most of the time, Mom's mind was somewhere else. Like when she watched the fruitcake dancing show on TV. He meant when the bubble show with Lawrence was on.

It was true. She would say, "Tommy, no questions during my show. Can I just have five minutes of peace and quiet? That's not too much to ask, is it?"

"Fruitcake" was one of Dad's sayings. He used it in the same sentence with his "light in the loafers," saying. I didn't know what it had to do with the bubble show. Mom said Dad called it that because he didn't appreciate music and couldn't dance.

Some of Mom's friends gave us fruitcake every Christmas. That was bad-tasting cake, and I even liked fruit. I learned to eat it, because a lot of times there was nothing else in the house to eat. When I would complain how bad it was, Mom would break out with her "eat it, and thank the good Lord you got it" saying. I never got hungry enough to thank the Lord for fruitcake. I did tell Mom to get me a pair of those light loafers so I could dance like that. She just laughed.

The only time I got my ears cleaned was during that show. Mom always sat in the big stuffed chair that had cotton sticking through the doilies on its arms. She would turn her apron around and have me lay my head across her lap. Her housedress was always damp and smelled of dish soap. Out would come a black bobby pin from her hair. With warnings not to move, she would stick the round end down into my ear.

At least once every time she cleaned my ears, she pushed the pin too far. Wow—that meant quick, hard pain. There was Mom with shaky hands, tired from working all day, watching TV. She was daydreaming that she was dancing with Lawrence Welk while he was directing the band. In the early years of his show, he sometimes chose a woman out of the audience to be his dance partner on stage. Later, when Bobby Burgess joined the show, Mom imagined herself as one of his partners. Through the years he had several. I was willingly allowing her to hold a bobby pin to my eardrum. I realized I had found my answer to "just how dumb is stupid?"

When Ronny was home, he always watched the bubble show with Mom. He'd sing the songs quietly to himself and never miss a note. Sometimes he had really bad days and talked through his nose, especially if he was tired or seemed nervous. Mom didn't like to talk about it; Dad never did. Dad would ignore him or tell him to keep quiet so as not to draw attention to himself. I think Dad was the one who didn't want the attention.

~~~

We were in the basement one day. I was watching Mom
~~~

wash clothes. Ronny sat on the damp cement floor not saying a word. He held paper up against the side of the washtub, and once again, he was writing something.

"Mom, why does Ronny talk the way he does?" I asked.

"It's because God made him that way."

"Why?" I asked.

"I think it's a test," she answered.

"Why would God need to test Ronny?"

"I didn't say the test was for Ronny," she replied.

"Who's the test for, then?"

"Tommy, just go out and play. No time for questions, I have to change the linen on the beds."

~~~

Sometimes during an argument, Dad left, and Mom kept talking. The night of the car-dealer incident was one of those times. Like I said, the drill had already started. Ronny was up in bed, and Dad was making him wait and think extra long. I was feeling good about beating old Blackie up the stoop.

Mom was in the kitchen, slamming pots and pans and saying, "That's right, be a husband and father last and always a cop first."

I think that was one of those grown-up sayings. Mom was saying one thing but meaning something else. She kept talking about how Dad should know things were not just black or white.

She looked toward the stairs and raised her voice a little. "There are gray areas too, no matter what you think!"

I don't believe he heard her or that she really wanted him to hear. Sometimes I think Mom was scared of Dad too.

It could have been a bad night for Ronny. His backside might have looked like a red reflector by the time Dad got tired of swinging and preaching. Stealing was a black-and-white thing, no in-between. No such thing as stealing just a little. You steal, you die. If he told Dad that I was with him, he'd miss out on any chance of killing me. Dad might put me on Boot Hill like the cowboys on TV. Even worse, in the graveyard across from the Ritz.

I was scared to death of that place. During the day it was
~~~

okay. On the way home from matinees, Ronny would read the gravestones to me. The one that bothered me the most was the one he would read in his deep, scary voice: "She is still alive."

When I was about seven years old, I fell asleep in the loveseat at the movies. It was two seats put together, with one pad—a perfect size for me to lie down on. It was also great for a boy and his girlfriend, unless big Sally showed up. She would make them move. I liked her. She would eat what she wanted of her popcorn and then hold it out in my direction. I would go over and grip the box with both hands.

She'd hold on tight and say in what Bobby said was proper English, "You're going to be a good little lad today. Say 'surely.'"

I would say "surely," and she'd tell me to go to the back, sit down, and keep quiet. She was way harder to understand than Ronny at his worst. I used to wonder how she knew I liked popcorn.

It was close to midnight before the janitor found me. Not a single person was left in the theater. Bobby and Ronny were with me when the movie started. They sneaked out and left me. They were probably still laughing, knowing that the only way home was walking past the graveyard. The shortcut was through the graveyard, but there was no way that was going to happen. They were going to be in big trouble when I told Mom. Dad was working at his second job that night. Sometimes for extra money he sorted mail in the train boxcars. Mom couldn't come pick me up because Dad never let her learn to drive.

I started the walk home. It was only about ten blocks, but four blocks of the sidewalk were right next to tombstones, statues of dead people, and scary-looking angels. I was so glad that Mom let me have taps put on my shoes two weeks earlier. They cost a quarter. She almost said no because of the money and because my heels were rubber. She said the tap nails wouldn't hold in rubber. She was right. My left tap was already hanging off the back of my heel.

Taps were to make the bottoms of shoes last longer. I got them because they sounded cool, but by the time I was next to the first headstone, they were hot. The only thing that was moving faster and louder was the beating of my heart. I slowed down, thinking that if I dragged my taps to make noise, acting like I wasn't scared, nothing would get me. It was cold. Mom had put Bobby's beanie hat on me before we left for the movies. If it was lost, it served him right for leaving me. He probably took it off my head while I was asleep in the loveseat.

My face and hands had gotten really cold. I pulled my wool socks out of the pockets of my peacoat. The coat was missing all but the top button. They had come up missing during Ronny's use. I wanted the button to be in the middle, but Mom said top was best because it kept my neck and shoulders warm. The coat had started out with my oldest brother, Jimmy. My mom had bought it used at a church rummage sale, and it had been handed down through the boys for years. I believe my oldest sister even wore it. It was big on me, but I would just roll the sleeves up a couple times.

Socks were my mittens all through elementary school. I always took them off before I reached the school grounds. I didn't want them to have to serve as boxing gloves too. After all, someone might say something truthful, like I was poor or looked stupid, or even worse, they might laugh at me.

My left tap finally came off. Ghost, or no ghost, I was not leaving my tap. I had to backtrack for at least ten graves, but I found my tap. It took me four or five tries to pick it up with my sock mitten on, but I got it.

I heard something and looked up. My tap had fallen off right in front of the "She is still alive" grave site. Arms on my chest, I started faking a whistle through the sock-mittened knuckles on my cheeks. Someone or something in the graveyard was following me.

I started thinking that maybe it was Headless Hattie's grave. After all, she was still alive and looking for a new head. That was a bedtime story my oldest sister used to tell me. The only thing that separated me from Hattie was a four-foot iron fence. The one tap and the fake whistle weren't working. It was time to run.

I yelled out, "No, Hattie, no!" and took off, making it all the way home and into the back door before stopping. I almost quit at the end of the street, but old Blackie was there to help me pick it up. I was actually glad to see that old dog.

It was a few months back that my sister had told my dad I had stolen her fountain pen. I couldn't read most words in regular print, much less in cursive. But her writing sure looked pretty, with curly capitals and circles for the dots over the letters *I* and *J*. I only wanted to see if I could write or spell better using a fountain pen. All she had to do to get the pen back was hide the ink bottle. I had only borrowed the pen for a few weeks, and I had to refill it at least every other day.

The back of my head still has a flat spot with a small bump where Dad's Masonic Temple ring landed.

On the kitchen floor with my fingers interlocked behind my head, I rolled back and forth from one elbow to the other.

Dad started in on me. "Do you know how many of your kind are in jail because they borrowed something that didn't belong to them?"

My head was killing me, and I didn't understand the question. I didn't want to give the wrong answer. I knew that people borrowed things that didn't belong to them. If they had it already, they wouldn't need to borrow. This could have been a trick question or just another saying. It was not the time to ask Dad to explain.

"I don't know. A hundred maybe?"

"No, it's hundreds, thousands, but if you steal again, you won't live to be one of them."

Ronny didn't know that stealing equaled death in my case. On the night of the car-dealer caper, I prayed he didn't tell Dad that I was anywhere near a reflector.

Dad finally opened the bedroom door and walked in yelling. "Stealing, taking something that doesn't belong to you, something that someone else had to work and pay for!" He slammed the door.

Right then, "at the drop of a hat," was a good time for Ronny to start crying. I had heard Mr. Katz, a neighbor, say that saying to his son. His son could hardly skate from one sidewalk crack to the next without falling and hurting or skinning something. One day his roller skate came off his shoe, right in front of his house. This time he didn't fall and bite the cement as usual, but he still started crying.

I reached down to give him my skate key when Mr. Katz called out, "What's wrong with you now? You cry at the drop of a hat. Get in this house, you big sissy!"

The boy walked with one skate on, the other dragging at the side of his ankle. The closer he got to his front door, the harder he cried.

My brother Bobby met me at our doorway. "Was that the 'sympathy boy' next door crying again?" he asked.

I ducked down to the side and slid between him and the door. "Mom, Bobby's making up names for people again," I said.

"Bobby, why do you have to place a label on everyone?" she asked.

"I don't. They label themselves. Look, the chubby, soft little boy cries. Mommy feels sorry for him and says, 'Let's get you an ice cream cone. You'll feel better.' As his dad said, he cries 'at the drop of a hat,' gets more ice cream from Mommy, gets chubbier, and may never learn to skate. A lot of sympathy may not be all that good. Empathy, now that's a whole different thing."

"What's empathy, Bobby?" I asked.

"It's something I don't have for you. Look it up."

It seemed like after a few months, no one remembered the boy's real first name. Everyone called him Sissy Katz. Not just Sissy or Katz, always both names. Most of the neighbor kids didn't play with him or weren't allowed to. It had something to do with his family not believing in Jesus. His name was Homer, and I always called him Homer.

I liked Homer, chubby or not. He was my age, and smart in reading and spelling. He could add numbers up really fast too. He always had money. At Johnny's Delicatessen, if I couldn't pay—which was most all of the time—he would say, "Go ahead, Tommy. Pick out something you like."

He'd say it just like a grown-up. Even if I picked out something that cost a lot of money, like a root beer and a candy bar, it didn't matter. One time my stuff cost more than Homer had in his pocket, and Johnny still gave us the candy.

"Would you put it on my mom's account?" Homer asked. "Sure."

We were halfway out the door when Johnny yelled, "Hey, Sissy Katz, come sign the tab!"

On the way home I asked Homer how I could get one of those account tabs. When I went up to the delicatessen to get things for Mom, if I didn't have the money, Johnny wouldn't give me the stuff. Homer said the account belonged to his mom and that I wasn't old enough to get one. I sure could have used one of those. The older boys on the block said Homer was a momma's boy and that's why he got to use the tab. I thought it was because he was smarter and understood his parents' sayings better.

"Homer, why do you answer people when they call you Sissy?"

"I don't know, Tommy. I think you're my only real friend."

"So?"

"Well, when people are calling me Sissy Katz, at least they're calling me."

I told my mom what he said.

"Be nice to Homer," she told me. "He needs a friend like you."

I thought maybe he needed to live with Ronny for a few weeks to help him toughen up a little.

I beat Homer most all the time in penny pitching, jacks, tiddlywinks, blind man's bluff, and steal the bacon—to name only a few of the games we played. Sometimes, I would let him win just so he wouldn't quit and go home. I only tried to teach him stickball once. The fact that he wore thick Coke-bottle type glasses didn't help him any.

Ronny got to where he didn't like to play games with us anymore. He said it wasn't fun because we were too easy to beat. So what? It didn't matter to us that he stopped playing. He had been writing during our turns most of the time anyway, and we had to remind him when it was his turn. He used to always tell me, "Keep your mind in the game. If you don't watch the shooter, he'll fudge, and you might lose all your marbles."

This would have been a good time to use that saying, "Practice what you preach," like he used on Dad.

Ronny found a cigar in Dad's coat pocket one day. After Dad walked out the door for work, Ronny got brave and said, "Practice what you preach." Of course I asked Mom if Dad smoked and showed her the cigar.

She read the paper ring on the cigar to me. "It's a boy." She explained that when a cop's wife had a baby, this was a way of letting the other policemen know.

"They could just tell them," I said.

"Oh no, then they couldn't sit around, smoke cigars, and talk about what a great job they did."

"Did doing what?" I asked.

"Making their firstborn come out a boy."

"Dad still has the cigar, so I guess he didn't smoke with the other cops," I said.

"That's right," she answered.

"So that means he didn't get to hear how great a job that cop did at making the baby."

Mom laughed.

Directly From You

Verse
I just dropped a couple nickels to check in with you
To see if what they're saying has any truth
My friend said your friend said you said we were through
But I need to hear it directly from you

Verse
They say one day you want me, the next day you don't
Tomorrow you should but you probably won't
That the way things are looking I just won't do
But I need to hear it directly from you

Chorus
Say it softly and gently to me
If the same lips that kiss me
And whisper they miss me
Are the same lips
That are saying we're through
I need to hear it directly from you

Verse
I just found the letter you put in my purse
Where you said that ya love me in verse after verse
What friends say is hearsay, and it just ain't true
I guess indirectly, that's directly from you

Chorus Repeat

Chapter 3
If You're the Way to Heaven
Rumor's Going Around
Will Tennessee What Arkansas
The Skinny, Freckled, Red-headed Girl

Reading was hard for me. The teachers said that I didn't hear or know my phonics, so they kept me back in the fourth grade an extra year. The same classroom with the three-inch chunk of the blackboard missing. The same desk with *Skip loves Sally* carved just below the empty inkwell hole. The same old teacher teaching in the same old clothes, telling the same old stories to the same old kids. They just had different names. The only thing that wasn't the same was the thermometer test.

Phonics. What did that mean? I could hear, and I could talk. It was the rules that I fought and couldn't understand. I wanted them changed, at least for me. The letter *I* worked when saying, "I'm going *into* the bathroom at the Norwood Waterworks Swimming Pool," but changed to an *E* on the *Enter* sign over the door. The beginning of both words sounded the same to me. It didn't make sense, or was it *scents* or *cents*? If something means something totally different, then make a word that sounds totally different. Forget about the "*I*-before-*E,* except-after-*C* rule." And the silent letter thing really bothered me. If a letter didn't make a sound, why use it? Why waste the time?

I overheard my teacher talking to the teacher across the hallway about me. She told her my middle name was "dumb." If it were, I wouldn't spell it with the letter *B* tagged on the end for no good reason at all.

My failing gave my brothers and sisters new ammo, but at least they quit with the "small runt" remarks for a while. After being teased all morning one day, I went outside and sat on the back doorstep, with my elbows on my knees.

Here came Ronny cutting across the neighbors' back yard. "Get out of the way, so I can get in," he said. "What have you been crying for?"

"Oh, nothing," I answered, as I sat back down.

While he closed the door, he said, "Don't start tapping your feet and faking a whistle through those knuckles on your cheeks."

It took me a few seconds, and then it hit me. I ran through the kitchen, jumped on his back in the dining room, and rode him into the living room. He started bucking and gulping back laughter, saying there was a flea on his back. He slung me onto the couch.

"That was you in the graveyard that night, wasn't it, Ronny?"

"Tommy, there's always someone in the graveyard."

"It was you, wasn't it?" I demanded.

"Why would you think it was me? Maybe it was, 'No, Hattie, no!'" he answered, in his whiny baby voice.

Now I knew it was him, and I started swinging. He put me into a headlock and took me to the floor.

"Ronny, you let him be!" Mom yelled from the other room.

I was thinking, *Let him be what? Strangled to death?*

He now had both hands around my neck, his cheek against mine, and his lips to my ear. "You got home okay that night, didn't you?" He pressed his lips against my temple, as if to kiss me, and released his hands. It took a few days for his red fingerprints to fade from my throat.

Looking back on the graveyard night, I realized that when I got home, Bobby was asleep in the big chair with the beanie hat lying on his chest, but Ronny was still not home. I guess maybe he was making sure I got home okay. At least that's what I want to think. The evil, scary stuff he did to me was one thing. The fact that he could go deep into a cemetery, walk on graves, and hide behind dead people's headstones was even scarier.

~~~

About a half hour had passed since Dad had slammed the
~~~

bedroom door, and there hadn't been another sound from the upstairs. I knew I wasn't going to hear Ronny crying or screaming, but I definitely thought the keys on the police belt would be jingling by then. There was still hope that Ronny hadn't told Dad that I was the spotter in the failed reflector caper. It was my job to find the biggest and best reflectors. Ronny's job was to take them off. My thumbs weren't strong enough to turn the wing nuts that held them to the license plates.

Dad, with his tricky police talk, might have been able to break Ronny down and make him spill his guts. My story was going to be that I only looked at the pretty reflectors, which was true. It was Ronny who actually took them. I felt bad, but this was do or die for me.

It was too quiet upstairs. I had to find out what was going on. I climbed on my hands and knees to the top landing, stopping every few steps to listen.

"Don't let him come out and catch you nosing around up there," Mom said quietly.

The night before, Dad had gone across the river into Covington to another one of those tent revivals. He had been going whenever he could over the past couple years. Mom said they were "just a bunch of holy rollers." She would go along sometimes merely to get out of the house. She had a good voice and liked the singing part of the meeting. Dad liked the preaching. He even took notes the couple times he took me. I liked it when the preacher talked loud and called us sinners. I always wondered what I had done wrong that he knew about.

I had turned around, still on all fours, and was now facing downstairs. In my soft voice, I told Mom that I couldn't hear anything and that Dad must still just be talking. Magically, from all the way down the hall, his foot was on my rear end. At least he pushed me sideways toward the wall and not down the stairs.

My forehead had landed on the radiator. It made more noise than pain. My bony head hit the loose iron grate on the hardwood floor. I was expecting a lot worse.

"You'll be okay," he said. "Now get to bed."

I was still alive. Ronny had held out, but he did take my milk money for the next two weeks.

"Don't you get in bed with those dirty feet," Mom said. "I just changed the sheets."

Too late. Bobby was down at the bowling alley, and my head was already on his pillow right next to Ronny. Ronny lay flat on his back with his hands behind his head, staring at the ceiling. I was surprised that he was able to lie on his butt. "Tell me, did he hit you even once?"

"No."

"Did he just talk all this time?"

"Yeah, more like preached."

"Did he bump your forehead with the heel of his hand and then raise it toward the sky?"

"No, Tommy."

"That's what the tent preacher does. What did Dad preach about?"

"He said that he's the way to heaven, that he's my heavenly road."

"What else?"

"That I could be absolutely stupid, and get along fine in this world if I'd only do what he says."

"I'm telling Mom, because she said Jesus was the only way. Ronny, do you think Jesus is the way to heaven, or do think it's Dad?"

"If it's Dad, it's going to be a hell of a way to go."

"I'm also telling Mom you're cursing again."

~~~

On the day we were going to ride in Dad's police car to check out the stool pigeon, Dad finally started walking back toward the car, and Uncle Lou finally stopped talking and said, "See you Saturday."

Dad yelled out, "Ronny, move over or get out and stay home! It's your choice."

It was about time. Ronny slid over, and I jumped in and started singing, "I was walking with my darling to the tennising walls, when an old friend I happened to see."

"What are you saying?" Ronny asked, choking back his laughter and smiling from ear to ear.
~~~

"I'm singing the 'Tennising Walls' song."

"Tommy, that song has been out for the past four or five years, and you don't know the words yet? It's not *walking,* it's *waltzing,* like dancing to a slow song. The waltz is named after the state of Tennessee, not tennising walls."

Dad got in, and Ronny stopped smiling. It was killing him not to laugh out loud. I could tell by the way he squinted his eyes and by the nose wrinkled upward, the pursed lips, and the ears moving.

Dad closed the door and cranked up the old, unmarked cop car. It was more fun riding in the patrol car with *POLICE* written on the side. The neighbor kids used to say how lucky I was and how cool it looked. Some of the policemen had just gotten brand new 1955 Chevy patrol cars. Being a plainclothes detective, Dad didn't want bad guys to know he was a cop. He had his gun in a shoulder holster under his suit coat and his badge in his wallet. I thought that if I were a cop, I'd show off my gun and badge.

He threw the spotlight on our house, turned on the siren, and put the red blinking light on the dash. He kept them on all the way down Mount Vernon Avenue. That was cool. What wasn't cool was that the *see* in Tennessee was spelled right and said right. The *saw* in Arkansas was spelled wrong and said wrong. We had been learning the state capitals in school that past week.

"Ronny," I asked, "Why does Little Rock, Arkansas, end with an *S* instead of a *W*?"

"It's spelled that way because the last part is Kansas, like the state of Kansas."

"Wow, now that really explains the *saw* sound for me."

"A little frustrated are we, Tommy?"

Was I ever? I needed to tell someone. "It's got me so frustrated, I'm bouncing off the walls at school. Look, Nashville, Tennessee, spells it right."

"Tommy, Nashville might even be the place where the song 'The Tennessee Waltz' or 'Tennising Walls,' as you like to sing it, was made. How did you ever come up with those words?"

"I'll tell ya later."

Dad had just quit talking with the dispatcher, and I didn't want him to hear. Ronny went back to writing, using his knee as a desk.

"So Dad, where is this stool pigeon?" I asked.

"Hopefully he's down at the corner of Third and Vine."

"What makes him different from the other pigeons?"

"He's my stoolie, my informant."

Before I could ask what an informant was, Ronny said, "It's a tattletale."

"So this pigeon can talk?" I asked.

"He sings like a bird," Dad said.

I remember thinking, *Okay, a male pigeon, with some kind of a tail, and it can sing like a bird.* I don't remember where, when, or how old I was before learning the difference in the spelling of *tail* and *tale.* "Pigeons are birds. Of course they can sing," I said.

"Tommy, he's a snitch, and this drunken old man sitting on the curb is probably him," Ronny said.

"That's a stool pigeon?"

The sad, dirty, unshaven man in a grease-spotted trench coat wore a hat that was too small for his head. The brim was torn and separated from its crown at the front. The Third Street and Vine sign shook from him sitting back rocking against its pole.

Dad pulled up alongside him and rolled the window down.

The old man was whining, talking to himself, and he smelled bad too.

"What's going on, Charley?" Dad asked.

"She got married on me, Chief."

Dad was only a detective, but the man called him chief. I had heard others on the street call him chief too.

"Dad, why's he calling you chief?"

"Chief is a semi-respectful way of telling me that I'm old, but still the boss." He turned to the man. "Charley, are you talking about your ex?"

"Chief, the rumor was going around that she still loved me, that she still cared. They even said she was coming back to me. Chief, I know there was no reason to believe it would work again, but I heard the rumor."

He started rocking more and made groaning sounds. He pulled out a bottle of wine from under his coat and started chug-a-lugging. Dad got out of the car and grabbed hold of his hands. They were the only thing that looked like a pigeon's. The twisted, clawed fingernails dug into the label as Dad slowly lowered the bottle down to Charley's waist.

"She's been gone a long, long time Charley. Maybe that's all it is—just a rumor."

This was the stool pigeon informant that sings like a bird, who was now crying like a baby? Dad grabbed his stoolie by the lapels of his coat, pulled him to his feet, and helped him stumble backward across the sidewalk. He pushed him back up against the brick wall of the corner bar and let him go. As the man slid down the side of the building, he dropped his bottle and sat there in a puddle of Mogen David and broken glass.

"I need to have something by tomorrow," Dad said. He took out a couple bucks, put them in the coat pocket of the "informant who knew nothing," and got back into the car and cranked it up. "Charley, are you gonna be okay?"

Tears ran down the man's cheeks. He licked his upper lip and sniffed snot back into his nose. "Chief, how can I be okay with this faded, broken life of mine? She's climbing the ladder of success."

"Charley, you made your choice. You should be happy for her and wish her the best." Dad took his foot off the brake and started rolling away. "Sober up and get me some info by tomorrow."

"It's not fair, Chief. I've got nothing, and she's got nothing but the best."

I sat back and put my feet on the back of the front seat for balance. I had landed on the floor from a quick right turn on the way there.

"That guy is nothing but a bum and a wino," Ronny said.

"Yeah," I added. "He wasn't nice to his wife, and he smelled."

"Tommy, never judge an Indian till you've walked a mile in his moccasins," Dad said.

First of all, none of the things I'd been told or led to believe were even close to true. The stool pigeon was not a pigeon; he could not, or did not, sing like a bird; he had no tail; and he had no information to be an informant. Now Dad wanted me to believe he was an Indian? He looked more like an old, dirty Lone Ranger without a mask than a Tonto. However, I didn't see what kind of shoes he was wearing.

Ronny said, "You're always telling us, 'Don't smoke. It'll stunt your growth and keep you from running fast. Don't drink. It'll make you crazy and make you do things you'll be sorry for later.' The snitch is just going to go buy more wine with that money."

"Dad, Ronny's right." I used one of Mom's sayings. "He *is* going to take that 'good, hard-earned money,' and spend it on wine."

Dad simply replied, "Tommy, maybe that's all he's got to keep him warm at night."

As soon as we walked in the back door, Mom said, "Straight upstairs and into the tub."

Ronny and I still took baths together when it was cold out. The water heater never worked—that is, if we even had one. We would only run a couple inches of water from the faucet. Mom would pour in a pot of boiling hot water from off the stove to warm us up. I sat in the front because Ronny's legs were longer. I hated that because sometimes he would pee on my back. By the time I knew he was smiling, it was too late.

He started smiling early that night as he asked again about the "Tennising Walls" song. "Really, Tommy, what made you think that those were the words?" "Promise you won't tell anyone?"

"Of course not," he said.

"Well, when we lived across town in Evanston, I'd go down to Walnut High School and watch the girls play tennis. They hit the balls off the big cement walls, and sometime they'd sing that song as they twirled their tennis skirts around."

"Were you too busy looking at their legs and their chests in those tight sweaters to understand what they were singing?"

"No, but now I'm thinking the teachers might be right. Maybe I don't hear the phonics. That should start with an *F* and not a *P*."

"No, Tommy, you just didn't hear the words well and did it by association."

"Did it by what?"

"Nothing. Don't worry about it. Just learn the right words."

"Ronny, you said you wouldn't tell, right?"

"Right. Tell what?"

"Tell about the legs and chest thing. Ronny, does it make you feel kind of funny when you look at girls?"

"Does it make you feel funny, Tommy?"

"Maybe not funny, but different. Two of them smiled at me, and I think they liked me."

"Tommy, the girls on the tennis team are upperclassmen. They won't even give guys my age the time of day."

"I wasn't asking for the time. I just wanted to watch."

That was another thing I didn't understand—words that are spelled the same and sound the same, but can mean two completely different things, like *watch*.

Ronny never really answered my question. I think he liked girls. I walked in on him lying on the couch, kissing our cousin. Dad always referred to her as the "skinny, freckled, red-headed girl." He could never remember her name. It was Ethylene, rhymed with gasoline, easy for me to remember. Skinny, freckled, red, or not, it looked like he was enjoying the kiss, but I didn't think she liked it. She was sticking her tongue out. I kept quiet and watched my cousin's tongue wiggle, while her forehead was sweating. She was a couple years older and able to stay on top of him, but Ronny was still stronger. Every time she'd get her butt up off of him, he was able to pull her right down again. When they finally saw me, they jumped up. They said they were playing a game called spin the bottle. I didn't see any bottle. I didn't know why they would waste time spinning it anyway—they were the only two playing.

My cousin was really worried that Uncle Lou would give

Ronny a beating if I told him what they were playing. If I were Ronny, I'd have been worried about *her* telling. She was the one he kept from getting up and made her sweat, slobber, and lose her breath.

Ronny had enough beatings. His last one before we moved from Cincinnati to Florida started at the coal yard. It was a Saturday afternoon, and Ronny and I were walking up Paxton Avenue to the delicatessen. Just across the road and behind the coal yard were the railroad tracks. They were the dividing line for the rich people of Hyde Park and us not-so-rich in Oakley.

Of course the train started slowing to a stop to pick up or dump off coal. Guess who decided to hop the train for a short little ride? Before I knew it, he was across the street and running alongside the train. He couldn't catch up and missed the boxcar handles on the first two tries.

Not good timing for Ronny. I kept walking toward the delicatessen, but I couldn't see Ronny anymore because Dad pulled the car up alongside me.

"Where's your brother?" Mom asked.

"We're going to try to trade these baseball cards for some candy. Mom, do you think Johnny will still give me something for this 1952 rookie card of Mickey Mantle? It's like three years old."

The train's whistle blew, and Dad looked across to see Ronny hanging from a boxcar with one arm. Ronny started waving to me until he saw Dad running toward him. He jumped, hit, and rolled—a lot better from the train than I had from the truck. He rolled right back up onto his feet and took off running behind the piles of coal, with Dad right after him. I had no idea Dad could move that fast. He was old, like in his forties.

Mom missed the whole thing. She was in the front passenger seat and was turned, talking to me. Dad had gotten out and run back down and across Paxton Avenue, dodging traffic.

"Where did your father go?"

"He's over in the coal yard."

"Your brother is in enough trouble. He better not be

getting dirty playing in that coal."

"I'm sure he's not playing, Mom."

I looked down a couple blocks toward our street. There was Dad holding Ronny by the back of the neck, pushing him across the road back toward the house.

"Come on, Mom. Dad's walking Ronny home."

"What about the car?" she asked.

"You get the keys, and I'll close Dad's door—that is, unless you want to drive."

"Don't get smart, Tommy. It's your father's fault that I can't drive. He'll do anything to keep me closed up in that house. I'm nobody's slave, and I'm tired of being treated like one."

To use another one of Mom's sayings, I sure opened "a can of worms."

"Why did you say that Ronny was already in enough trouble?" I asked.

"Your father found out that he's been going over to Clarence's house again. You know how your father feels about him."

"Come on, Mom. Walk faster."

Mom was the buffer between Dad and Ronny. With Ronny jumping the train and being over at Clarence's house, he could already be dead. I never really understood why Dad didn't like Clarence. He never called him by his name. It was always "the fruit from down the street."

Clarence was no longer a teenager but still dressed like one. He dressed a little like a "hood," wearing motorcycle-type boots with pegged-leg Levi's. He kept a pack of Lucky Strikes rolled up in the sleeve of his T-shirt, and his pocket watch hung from the end of a shiny, big-looped dog chain. He had a high voice and a little hissing sound at the end of some words, but boy could he sing pretty. He was really good at playing musical instruments too. He could play piano, saxophone, clarinet, and guitar.

Ronny really loved music. At least he wanted to. Clarence said that Ronny was a natural and that he had an ear for it. Not an extra ear—he meant that he could hear the notes. Ronny could learn stuff fast. He knew the words to every song that came on the radio. Clarence was willing to teach him how to play for free, but Dad said he wasn't teaching his kids anything. Ronny gave up trying to get Dad to let him play the piano or buy a guitar.

Mom and I reached the front porch and stayed out there.

Dad and Ronny were talking really loud, but at least they were still only talking.

"He's never tried anything but to teach me music," Ronny yelled through his mouth and nose.

"You stay away from him; he's as queer as a nine-dollar bill."

I could hardly wait to ask Ronny about that saying.

Dad came out, slammed the door, and in his anger asked, "Where's the car?"

"Mom was going to drive it home, but I stopped her," I said, jokingly.

"She better not try to drive that car!"

Mom tossed—or I should say threw—the keys at him as he started walking back up Mount Vernon Avenue.

"Sorry, Mom. I almost got you in trouble."

"You didn't get me in trouble. I'm not afraid of your father. He doesn't tell me what to do. He might be your boss, but he's not mine!"

Oh no, more "worms."

That night in bed I asked Ronny, "What about the 'nine-dollar bill' thing?"

"Have you ever seen one?" he asked.

"No. Have you?"

"Of course not, Tommy. There is no such thing. That's why it would be queer if you had one."

"But why would Dad say Clarence is as queer as one? He *is* real, and you can see him."

"It means that he's refined, polished, and maybe a little effeminate."

"Ronny, those are all big words. I think it just means he doesn't have a girlfriend yet."

"Go to sleep, Tommy."

"Ronny, you should put your undershirt on. Mom says that the 'night air will get you.'"

~~~

The first ten years of my life were divided between the two neighborhoods of Evanston and Oakley in Cincinnati, Ohio. It wasn't long after my parents started talking about moving to Florida that we were on the road. Ronny and I did get to ride in the truck one more time, to give our furniture to Uncle Lou. From selling the house and money from the police department, Dad bought a two-door, 1955, green-and-white Pontiac.

Everyone in the neighborhood came over to say goodbye and to congratulate my parents on the new car. It was a big deal back then. Dad was proud, telling one and all that the car was only a few months old and that it had low mileage. He used the "as good as new," saying. Even Clarence showed up. He had his shirt collar turned up and wore a new hairdo with a lot of Brylcreem. The sides were combed straight back. I overheard Dad tell Mom that the back of his head looked like a duck's ass. I looked, and it did.

Clarence also said his goodbyes because we were leaving early the next morning. I liked him, and Mom thought he was nice too. We all watched as Ronny walked with him down the street a few houses. Clarence put his arm around Ronny's shoulders, gave him a little hug, and rubbed the top of his red head. As soon as Dad started to walk toward them, Clarence crossed the street, head down, and waved goodbye without turning around.

Dad mumbled, "That fairy thinks he's that Elvis Presley kid we saw on *The Ed Sullivan Show* last week."

At the time I thought, *Why not try to be like Elvis? You sure don't want him to be who he is.*
~~~

If You're the Way to Heaven

Verse
You said I'd hear the music from the harps the angels played
That the streets were paved in gold, babe, all along the way
You have been dishonest I want you to know
If you're the way to heaven it's a hell of a way to go

Chorus
If you're the way to heaven it's a hell of a way to go
You tell me to stay on course, that you're my heavenly road
If you'd look a little closer at the smile on my face
You'd see it's only the upside down of a frown I can't erase
The devil makes me love you, the good Lord lets me know
If you're the way to heaven it's a hell of a way to go

Verse
I know I'm not as pretty (handsome) as I used to be
Time has been much kinder to you, babe, than it's been to
 me
I know that I'll forgive you because I love you so
But if you're the way to heaven it's a hell of a way to go

Chorus Repeat

Rumor's Going Around

Verse
I've heard you've climbed the ladder of success
That all you have is nothing but the best
Even though you've married and you're a lady of leisure
    time
The rumor's going around that you're still mine

Verse
Years have passed and I am a patron of the streets
Where I watch man grow from self-pity to defeat
I can't build the future on hearsay or make-believe
But the rumor's going around that you're still mine

Chorus
Oh, the rumor's going around that you still love me
The rumor's going around that you still care
Rumor's going around that you're coming back to me
But there's just no reason to believe it'll work this time

Verse
If you should show at the corner of Third and Vine
And find an old man there drunk from the taste of wine
Please don't tell him that the rumor is a lie
I believe it's the only reason he's still alive

Will Tennessee What Arkansas

Verse
I'm sitting here in Little Rock with elbows on my knees
Faking a whistle through the knuckles on my cheeks
You upped with him to Nashville having a ball
But the question is, will Tennessee what Arkansas?

Chorus
Will it thunder in his head from the lightning in your eyes?
Will his heart be heavy from the tears you'll make him cry?
Will his life be shattered from the whirlwind that you'll
    cause?
Yeah, the question, is will Tennessee what Arkansas?

Verse
I'm sipping on a paper cup; your lipstick's on the rim
Trying to figure out why you dumped me for him
It's got me so frustrated I'm bouncing off the walls
Yeah, the question is, will Tennessee what Arkansas?

Chorus Repeat

Skinny, Freckled, Red-Headed Girl

Verse
Yeah you can get caught with mud in your eye
Your foot in your mouth and your thumb in the pie
But don't get caught with the skinny, freckled, red-headed
 girl
Yeah you can get caught with your hand in the till
In the cookie jaw and telling fairytales
But don't get caught with the skinny, freckled, red-headed
 girl

Chorus
Because she's my girl
And she's got just what it takes
To make a man feel good
Like only a woman could
Oh don't get caught
With the skinny, freckled, red-headed girl

Bridge
If you wanta live to be a ripe old age
If you wanta live to see another day
You can get caught being bad in school
Skippin' class break the golden rule

But don't get caught with the skinny, freckled, red-headed
 girl

Chorus repeat

Chapter 4
Don't Let This Old Heart

Dad had taken early retirement, and we were going to live with our grandparents for a while. His father, the only grandpa I'd heard of, owned the ABC Garbage Company in central Florida. It was growing, and he was getting too old to handle all the customers, so Dad was going to take over and build the garbage business. He had left Florida at the age of seventeen almost thirty years earlier, hitchhiking north. He stopped and worked the farms along the way for room and board and ended up in Cincinnati a year later. Ironically, he met my mom at a dance. I'm sure he was the "wallflower." Instead of asking her to dance, he asked her to marry him, and that's how the story began.

The morning after saying our goodbyes, we drove off before the neighbors were up, or even the sun. Ronny and I were quiet and sad. Bobby was quiet and mad. He was sixteen and leaving school, friends, job, and a girlfriend. He sat by the window and put a pillow on the side of his leg between us. I thought that was nice, a place for me to lay my head. When I had barely touched the pillow, he slugged me in the kneecap and informed me that I wouldn't recognize my leg by the time we got to Florida—that is, if I continued to touch the pillow. I didn't know a bone could hurt so much.

Dad, my little sister, Nancy, and Mom were in the front. My sister Norma attended nursing school, and my brother Jimmy worked for a milling machine company. They stayed in Cincinnati, and Dad said they were on their own.

Norma had brought Mildred home, back when I was only six. Mildred was about four years old at the time we moved to Florida. We didn't know what kind of dog she was. Mom would laugh and say she was a "Heinz 57" ketchup variety.

From what I understood, Dad wasn't happy with my

sister's surprise. Mildred ended up liking Ronny more than my sister or anyone else. Ronny always made sure that she had water and something to eat. If it was cold, rainy, or too hot out, he made sure she was at least down in the basement. I can't remember her ever having dog food, only table scraps or part of Ronny's supper. He taught her tricks and talked to her like she knew what he was saying. When he asked her questions, Dad told him how stupid he sounded, and that he was "dumber than the dog" because he waited for her to answer.

When it came to Mildred and Florida, Ronny was right. Dad had planned to leave Mildred with my aunt and uncle. I had wondered why Dad had been so nice to her the day before. He allowed her to ride with us in the truck on the last load. He let her out at Uncle Lou's, put her in the back yard, and told her to go play. We had only brought the bed frames with us because my aunt had said that she didn't want our "urine mattresses," and that we were to leave them there in the house when we left for Florida. Ronny and I put the frames into their garage.

When Dad went into the house to talk to my aunt and give her back the truck keys, Ronny went around the far side of the house. A few minutes later he came running, holding Mildred. He put her in the back of the car on the floor under his legs and told her to lie down. I asked what he was doing, and he said, "Keep your mouth shut and get in the front!" Wow, I wondered what he had done that was so bad that he would let me ride shotgun.

Dad came out, got in, cranked up the car, and waved to my aunt. "Tell Lou and the kids goodbye for us," he yelled. "Make sure you come to Florida for a visit next summer."

We made it out of the neighborhood and back onto Duck Creek Road before Dad heard Mildred growl. She didn't like Ronny holding her down. Dad screamed, "Is that damn dog in this car?" and slammed on the brakes right in front of the Big Boy hamburger restaurant. That was the burger I wanted but never got to taste.

He opened the door, got out, and pulled the back of the front seat forward. He grabbed Mildred by the fur of her neck and threw her across the parking lot. Ronny flew out of the backseat. He had one foot halfway out the door when Dad met him with a full left hook to the middle of his chest. It knocked him to his stomach across the backseat. Dad got back in the car and closed his door. I was crying after hearing the sound of Dad's fist against Ronny's breastbone. It looked like Ronny's whole body stopped still for a few seconds when he landed on the seat.

Dad backhanded me in the jaw when I started begging him to go get Mildred. I didn't understand why or what he was doing. Before I could even get my hand to my mouth to check for lost teeth, Ronny pushed the back of my seat up. My forehead and left eyeball smashed into the dashboard. He opened the door, slid out sideways, and took off toward Mildred. I had blood running from my eye down my neck and onto my shirt.

By the time Dad quit worrying about my blood getting on his new car seat, Ronny and Mildred were gone. We circled Big Boy's and drove around the area for a long time.

"Where do you think he went?" Dad asked.

"I think he's kicking bull-pucky down the road."

I had heard my uncle say that saying to Dad a few days before, about him retiring. He said, "Well, Jim, it won't be long, and you'll be kicking bull—"

Before I could take another breath, Dad had slapped me hard on the back of the head twice. I swear my eyes went crossed.

I noticed that Dad was acting a little different. We couldn't find Ronny. Dad's hands were shaking like Mom's did most of the time. I knew Ronny had Mildred, and I also knew he could take care of himself, so I asked if we could get a hamburger. Dad looked at me but didn't answer. No matter, I could see the answer out of my right eye as the burger sign got smaller in the mirror.

"Tommy, don't grow up to be like your brother. Look at the trouble he's caused, and we need to leave early in the morning."

"Mom told me to always love others even if they're bad sometimes. Dad, do you love Ronny even when he's bad sometimes?"

He looked at me but didn't answer, again. He quickly pulled over in front of a liquor store and told me to stay in the car while he used the phone to call the police station.

We got back to the house but without Ronny or Mildred. Dad took his red, bloodstained handkerchief from my hand and threw it into the garbage as we walked in the back door.

"What happened to you, and where is Ronny?" Mom asked.

Before I could tell on Dad, he told me to go straight up to bed.

The only thing left in the room was the mattress on the floor and our clothes in shopping bags. The mattress was bare—no sheets, just mom's old quilt that had memories. The quilt lay at the top of a flat pillow with no pillowcase.

It wasn't long before Mom showed up with one of her famous cold dish towels. She came into the room and slammed the door. "You go and read the Good Book now, Jim," she yelled through the closed door. "You can be a Bible-thumper, but you should try living it, instead of just quoting it."

Mom laid the towel on my eye and moved my head over. The sore spot from dad's double slap shot pressed right on one of the mattress buttons. I quickly turned my head to the side, putting cheek, lips, and nose on an old, smelly pee stain.

"Mom, is *urine* the name of our mattresses?"

"No, you silly thing. Urine is another name for pee."

"Oh."

"Why would you think that? Haven't you ever heard that word before?"

"I thought it was like the names Barq's and Hires are for root beer."

"Why would you think that?"

"Because Aunt Helen said she didn't want our urine mattresses."

"She said that?"

"Yes."

"Why, that snotty little ungrateful thing. I'd like to make

her eat this mattress! Try to go to sleep now, Tommy."

Mom must have really been mad at Dad to have said something like that about someone. Usually she would have said one of her sayings, like, "Tell your aunt not to look a gift horse in the mouth."

Ronny gave up trying to explain the counting of teeth in a horse's mouth to me. I told him, even if the horse was a gift, I'd want to know if it were any good or not. He said I would figure that saying out when I got older. Then he told me that I would be missing some teeth and that I might not live long enough to figure that saying out if I asked him another question.

I lay there on the mattress thinking about the last few hours. The only reason that I had ridden in the truck with the last load was to get to ride back home in the new car. Mom had said, "Just stay home. You'll be sick of that car by the time we get to Florida."

I looked back on what I would have missed out on, had I listened to her. I would have missed a sore jaw, a bloody cut through my left eyebrow, a dent in my forehead, another stamp of Dad's ring on the back of my head, and the experience of going cross-eyed. Oh yes, plus the bonus of riding in the front seat. It was then that I started to realize that Mom was a whole lot smarter than she got credit for being.

Ronny always had trouble with wetting the bed. Mom said he was a "hard sleeper." Many times I can remember Dad spanking him for not getting up in the middle of the night to go to the bathroom. Dad made him wear a diaper to bed for a while when he was as old as ten. It made him feel really bad because Dad told all the neighbors and our relatives.

Ronny never showed anger like I would have, had Dad done that to me. Ronny was able to let it go, but he became a little quieter, stayed to himself, and wrote a little more. I asked Ronny why he didn't say anything to Dad about doing that to him. He said, "It wasn't worth the trouble for the problem it would cause." I told Ronny, I liked that saying, using "trouble and problem" in the same sentence. They can mean the same, but he used one to tell about the other. Ronny said it wasn't a saying.

I heard Mom call out, "Thank ya, Jesus! Thank you!"

Dad's ex-partner had showed up with Ronny and Mildred.

"Get upstairs," Dad told Ronny, using his tough voice. "You'll pay for this later!"

Bobby was still out with his friends. He had gone to the bowling alley to say goodbye to his boss. His "supposed-to-have-been" girlfriend Barbara had broken up with him a week earlier. They had a little argument, and now she wasn't talking to him. Bobby had no clue as to why.

"Mom, why couldn't Barbara just be nice another week so they could kiss goodbye?" I asked. I had seen them kiss before.

"Tommy, the argument was so she didn't have to kiss him goodbye."

"I don't understand that."

"Someday you will, Tommy. Someday you will."

Bobby didn't sleep with us in the same bed anymore. He had bought an army cot from the Army Navy Surplus Store. He paid for it with his bowling job money after his first two paychecks.

Ronny came in and lay down next to me. Most of the time he would still make me lie with my head toward the end of the bed and would give me a kick if any part of my body accidentally touched his. But not that night. Ronny laid his head next to mine on the pillow with the side of his arm touching mine. I was ready for him to tell me to "move it or lose it," but he didn't. He just lay there looking up at the ceiling.

"Ronny, is Mildred okay?"

"She's okay."

"Do you think Dad will let her go to Florida with us tomorrow?"

"Tommy, I couldn't believe my ears. Mom just told Dad in no uncertain terms that if Mildred doesn't go, she doesn't go. She said, 'Please don't let this old heart hear you say goodbye. But if you say goodbye to Mildred, you're saying goodbye to me.'"

"Wow, Mom was really mad earlier too."

"Oh crap, I have to go," Ronny squealed. "I don't want to piss the bed!"

"I don't think Mom will care if you do. She wants to make Aunt Helen eat this mattress anyway. In no uncertain terms. Ronny what does—"

"Not tonight. We have a long ride tomorrow."

"Do you want me to get you a cold dish towel for your chest bone?"

I know he heard me, but he didn't answer. By the time I got back with the towel he was asleep, and the mattress was wet. I wondered if he had peed on purpose. When I got up to go get the cold towel, his ears were moving, which means he was smiling. It was the last chance to sleep with my head at the top of the mattress. Instead I had to go to the bottom to find a dry spot.

~~~

By the time we crossed the Ohio River, Mom was crying. Maybe she knew we wouldn't be coming back even for a visit. Mildred was already asleep on the floor at Ronny's feet behind the driver's seat. Bobby told Ronny to put his shoes back on because his feet smelled worse than the dog. Bobby was right. But he wasn't right about Uncle Lou.

"I'm going to miss Uncle Lou," I said.

"You're going to miss him because he 'pro-pitches' to you."

"He's no pro pitcher. I know every player on the Cincinnati Reds, and he's not one of them."

"I mean he's a propitiator, you screwball," Bobby said. "You like him because he gives you things like candy to win you over."

"Mom, Bobby's giving Uncle Lou a label that I don't understand."

"Tommy, don't start. Bobby, please don't get him wound up."

I just knew this was going to be a great learning trip. I had Ronny trapped with Mildred on my left, and Bobby sleeping and/or daydreaming of his girl on my right. Bobby
~~~

was a better informant than Dad's stool pigeon. He liked to "inform" us of things. Like before we even backed out of the driveway, he informed me about touching the pillow. Of course, it was after he knocked my kneecap out of place.

He always used big words when he talked to me and Ronny. When I asked him what a word meant, he said the same thing my teachers said. "Look it up in the dictionary."

Of course my answer was, "If I knew how to spell it, I would."

Ronny usually took the time to tell me the meaning of a word. About a couple hours into the trip, I asked him if he wanted me to hold Mildred for a while. She had only been going from the floor to Ronny's lap that whole time.

"Let me inform you that there will be grave consequences if any part of that dog passes over the midline of the car," Bobby said.

Bobby had changed from "skinny and lanky" to "lean and wiry." At least that's what Mom had informed us.

"Just what and where is midline?" I asked.

He reached out with his long, wiry arm, which still looked skinny to me, and pointed. His bony finger informed me. "It runs from the middle of the dashboard through the space between the front seats. Most importantly is that it continues to right about where your forehead is and where my fist will land. Now, if the dog should actually touch me, then my fist will land on your numbskull brother over there."

"I don't see any line," I said.

"It's imaginary, yet oh-so-real," he replied.

"Will you be using your right wiry arm or your left still-skinny arm?" I asked.

"You don't need to know, you little runt."

"Why don't I?"

"Because it'll happen so fast you won't see it coming. I also promise that you will feel the pain for a very long time."

"Is that all of the . . . how do you say . . . consequences?" I asked.

"Yes, and I assure you that they'll be ample."

"So how do I end up in the grave from a hit by you to my forehead? Look at my dent and my fresh scab over my eyebrow with the missing hair. The dashboard is much harder than your fist."

"No, Tommy," Ronny explained, "tough man over there is using the word grave to mean important and/or serious consequences."

Oh please, Lord, I thought. *Not another word that's spelled and sounds the same but can mean not only two, but three different things.* Right then I promised myself that when or if I ever learned to read better, the dictionary would be my first book.

The car was kind of quiet through the first part of Kentucky. Ronny looked out the window, singing the words written on the road signs. They didn't rhyme or make any sense. When he sang aloud to himself, his tongue relaxed, his voice softened, and the sound came out of his nose more than his mouth. Mom said this put him in his own little world.

I asked her where my little world was. She said she was sure I'd find it someday. I asked her if she had a little world. She was looking at Dad, and she wasn't smiling. "No," she said, "but I sure hope there are other worlds for me to sing in!"

Bobby had his head back and against the side of the car with the pillow hiding his face.

"Hey, how about you stop hogging the pillow and start sharing?" I said.

Mom turned around with her finger pointing up and across her pretty red lips. She quietly told me, "Leave him be."

"Why? I want to use the pillow too."

"Because sometimes love hurts, Tommy, and right now he's hurting."

I had Mom trapped. There was no better time to ask questions. "Mom, if love hurts, why do you tell me to love our neighbors, love others, and love our fellow man? That could end up being a lot of hurt. Is love just having a lot of like for someone, so they change the word? What is it exactly? What does the guy who wrote the dictionary say it is? Ronny told me I would know if I loved a girl by the thrill it would cause in my pants."

Dad turned to look at Ronny and almost went off the road. He swung and grabbed but couldn't reach him. My little sister was lying down asleep with her legs in Dad's lap. Ronny smiled big and choked back his laughter. He smiled not only because Dad couldn't get to him, but because he saw Mom smiling too. She was holding back laughing herself, hiding it from Dad. Every time he looked over at her, she had her nose and mouth in a napkin, shaking her head. I could tell she still thought it was funny. She had eyes like Ronny. When her mouth smiled, her eyes smiled. Her ears just didn't move.

"Young man, I've had all of you I can take, so if I were you, I would tuck it in," Dad said to Ronny in his quiet but meaning-it voice.

Ronny had laid his head back and pulled his Cincinnati Redlegs cap down over his face.

"*You* better hope that I don't have to pull this car over! Believe me I *won't* forget what you've said and done these past few days," Dad said, emphasizing the important words.

Ronny pinched me on the leg, lifted the bill of his cap, looked at me, and mouthed the words, "You dumb ass."

I didn't think "thrill in my pants" was funny like Mom did or bad like Dad did. I thought I'd have Ronny explain it better to me before we got to Florida.

I let a little quiet time go by. Mom had no house to clean, supper didn't have to be on the table by six, and there were no dishes or laundry to do. She couldn't tell me to go out and play, so I tried again.

"Mom, is there no way to tell or explain love? Does everyone feel or show it in different ways? Bobby said his stomach would flip over every time he saw his girlfriend. If a girl and I want to fall in love, is there a trick?"

She started out by taking a deep breath. "There is a trick to love, Tommy. I've found it to be a combination of a few things. It starts from the minute you and that young lady become infatuated with each other."

"Mom, he has no clue what that means," said the voice from under the baseball cap. "I don't even know what infatuation is."

Mom continued, "Okay, Tommy, the day will come that you start having strong feelings of attraction for a girl and hopefully her for you. The first thing is to take the time to get to know one another. Knowledge of a person is very important. God tells us in the Bible that in order to love him, we must know him. It's the same thing. In order to love her, you must get to know her. Learn to know what she likes and doesn't like. Learn the simple things that help her feel good about herself."

"That's a lot to remember," I said.

"Oh, there's more. Gain knowledge about her true feelings toward others. Hopefully she'll have a kind heart. If she does, she deserves to keep it. Don't belittle her; instead, say something nice to her every day. If for any reason you find her angry or with a broken heart, you need to be a peacemaker."

Mom had leaned over onto her armrest. She had been rubbing her shaky little hands together, but she still gave Dad the "you know I'm right" look. That was the one with head tilted, chin out, bottom lip up. "Tommy, as you share your past with each other, you may learn some 'lifesavers.'"

"I'd love to earn some lifesavers," I said.

Ronny had reached over to flick me on my ear right when I turned my head toward him. The nail of his middle finger flicked off his thumb at a hundred miles per hour, right into my dashboard eyebrow. It stung so bad, and it started bleeding again.

"She said *learn,* not *earn.* She's talking about things that can help save your married life, not candy." Ronny had pulled me over into his side under his arm with his hand over my mouth. "If you cry or scream you'll be sorry. Now get the napkin from Mom and make sure you don't get any blood on the car."

"What's going on back there?" Mom asked.

Ronny spoke up, while still squeezing my already sore jaw shut. "He hit his sore eye on my finger. Mom, let me hold that napkin on Tommy's eye for a few minutes with a little pressure."

Mom actually told Ronny that it was nice of him to be willing to do that for me. She never asked how my eyebrow ran into his finger.

"*Caring* is the next trick, Tommy. You care how she feels, if she's sick or if she's just physically worn out. You care about her emotions, if she's happy or if she's sad. You care if she feels that she just can't make it another day. You don't mentally knock her down and keep her living and working in emotional fear. No, you lift her up so she can be enthusiastic about her life and her purpose for existing. You let her know that her usually thankless job has merit; it has value. You tell her often that you couldn't make it without her. You help her because you're concerned and care for her well-being."

I started to ask Mom if she meant to say "her being well" instead of "her well-being." All I got out of my mouth was "Did you—" before Ronny poked me.

He had grabbed me by his most favorite spot, my neck, and pressed his mouth to my ear. "Shut up! Mom's on a roll. She's not talking to you. Just listen and learn something, you imbecile."

Imbecile, a new word that sounded nice but couldn't be, from the way he spat it into my ear. I planned to ask him later what it meant.

Bobby took his pillow down, pushed me forward, leaned behind me, and whispered to Ronny, "Wow, Mom's unloading. How long has this been bottled up?"

Dad kept driving, and Mom kept talking. She did turn her head toward the backseat, and she said my name a few times. So why wouldn't I have thought she was talking to me? After all, I'm the one who asked her all the questions.

Ronny had his pen and paper out again. Dad had made him put it away a couple hours ago because he got carsick from reading and writing. He threw up out the window, and the puke went all over the back side of the new Pontiac. I missed the barfing action with Ronny's head hanging out of the car. I woke up when Dad had pulled off on the side of the road and yanked Ronny out of the backseat by his ear.

"Isn't it amazing how the whole body will follow the ear

wherever it goes?" Dad said. He pushed Ronny away from the car and made him stick his finger down his throat. "Get all that crap out of you!"

Mildred jumped out and went to the bathroom. Just as Ronny heaved again, she stuck her head under the vomit.

"Get this damn dog out of here!" Dad yelled and tried to kick her.

Ronny got between Dad and Mildred. "Don't kick her! She didn't do anything. Kick me if you want. I'm the one that got sick. Don't kick her. Please don't!"

Dad stopped and told Ronny, "Take your socks off and give them to me."

We had a couple of Mason jars full of water. Dad got them out of the trunk and gave one to Ronny. "Rinse your mouth out and pour the rest on that dog's head and get back in the car. No more of that writing bull crap."

Dad took the other jar of water, and with Ronny's socks, washed the already chewed food off the back fender. We could hear "damn it" with every stroke.

Don't Let This Old Heart

Verse
Make no mistake, it's gonna break
I can tell by the ache
And the beat that it skips in the night
It's gonna crumble, gonna fall
Like Humpty Dumpty off the wall
If this old heart hears you say goodbye

Chorus
So say so long, see ya later after a while
Say you'll catch me on the flip side with a smile
Sneak out like a thief in the night
Just don't let this old heart hear you say goodbye

Verse
I started feeling really bad
With a cloud in my head
As the tears filled up in my eyes
If they fall they'll wipe me out
Like Itsy Spider up the spout
If this old heart hears you say goodbye

Chorus Repeat

Chapter 5
Kissy Face

We got back on the road, but I couldn't take it—Ronny's breath smelled so bad. I told Mom that I couldn't sit by him anymore because he was making me sick. He was facing me and breathing heavy. She gave him her whole last pack of Juicy Fruit gum. He put piece after piece in his mouth and chewed nice and slow. He kept saying how good it tasted.

"Come on, Ronny, give me the last piece," I begged.

"Oh no," he said, "it'll take the whole pack to smell just right for you. I wouldn't want you to get sick and not be able to sit by me."

"Mom, tell Ronny to share."

"Ronny, give him a piece of that gum."

"If only he had asked sooner."

"You're a liar! I did ask." About ten minutes down the road, I told him, "I think you were right, Ronny, about needing all five pieces of the gum. You sure do smell good now. I think that's my favorite gum."

"Really? Why is it your favorite?"

"Because it's juicy, it tastes like fruit, and it smells good too."

"Well, in that case, here." He pulled out a piece from under his leg and gave it to me. He hadn't chewed the whole pack after all.

That piece of gum tasted so good. I remember it being one of the happiest parts of the trip. I don't know if it was the taste of the gum or the fact that Ronny saved it for me.

"You're going to get in trouble if Dad catches you writing," I whispered. "If you throw up again, he'll make you walk to Florida."

"Then don't let him see me. Block the rearview mirror with that fat head of yours, and keep Mom talking."

"Okay." I spoke up so Mom could hear me. "Mom, if my girlfriend got a broken heart, I couldn't piece it back together, could I?"

"The word is *peacemaker*," Ronny said to me as if I were stupid. "*Peace,* like the opposite of war, not like pieces of candy." Then with his being-smart voice, he said, "No, Tommy, you're right. I'm wrong. You just pick up the pieces and put it back together."

"Is that true, Mom? If a heart is really broken, can it be fixed?"

She slowly looked over toward Dad. "Sometimes, Tommy, a heart can be broken into so many pieces that even a peacemaker can't fix it."

"Mom, are those all the tricks to love? Knowing, caring, and making sure you don't break her heart?"

"That would be a great start for a wonderful marriage, Tommy."

Ronny was writing on a homemade, stapled-together pad. It was made of half pages of lined school paper. He wrote on his knee, bent over behind Dad's seat.

Bobby had come alive and was staring at the back of Mom's head. He held his head up and opened his eyes a little wider when he really wanted to hear. He read more than he listened. His head was usually down, and he didn't look straight into people's faces when he talked to them. I think that was because he read too much with his head bent down. Mom had a saying for Bobby too. Whenever I asked where he was, she'd say, "Find the open book, and his nose will be stuck in it."

He had put the pillow back on the seat between us. "Now, runt, need I reinform you of the boundaries?"

I was going to say no, but Ronny spoke up. "Oh please, do tell. We wouldn't want to enter your precious space without permission."

"Well, runt, your wise-talking, crazy brother over there may be a little smarter than the world gives him credit for."

My little sister was three years old. When she wasn't sleeping, she stood up on the seat between Mom and Dad. One of them would keep an arm across her or an elbow on her belly. Hopefully this would keep her from flying through the windshield at sudden stops.

Mom pulled her down and sat her on her lap. She turned around in the seat and looked at us with her watery eyes. "We still have a long way to go. Please, no fighting or arguing. Bobby, you should know better."

"Mom, I was only going to give a story on territories so this little scholar could understand boundaries better. I'd use pictures for him if I had any."

Mom was too sweet.

While Dad was trying to find a preacher on the radio, he yelled out, "Shut the hell up back there!"

"Mom, how could we argue with Bobby?" Ronny said. "It's true he was only going to educate us on the meaning of boundaries."

"Okay, but keep it down," she said as she turned back around.

"Now, oh wise one, please go ahead," Ronny requested with a half-nose, half-mouth voice. "Continue with your definition of boundaries. Pick up from where you were before Mom so rudely interrupted your knowledgeable explanation."

Bobby was going to be seventeen next month and in his last year of high school. Ronny was going to be fourteen in a few months, and I had just turned ten. Bobby was real school smart. Mom said he had taken the smart test they called the IQ test and got a 135. She said he was no genius, but he was gifted. I had never heard of a test where you could get more than a 100. I never got even close to a 100, and a 135 would take a miracle. I always thought Ronny was the smartest. Maybe it was because we were closer in age. He and I were home more at the same time. He could and would answer my questions most of the time.

"Tommy, you see the pillow rolled up putting distance between our legs?" Bobby asked.

"Yes."

"It's the pillow that you must not even touch, if at all possible. It's the pillow that you must surely never cross over and touch me. You understand pictures, stories, and make-believe better than the written word, right?"

"I do?" I asked.

"Of course you do!"

"I guess you're right. I do like stories and the movies better than trying to read a book."

"Tommy, I want you to think of this pillow as a river. Let's give it a name. We'll call it the Rubicon River. Though it's very small, it's of great importance."

"Is this story going to be a good one?" I asked. "I mean, like is there going to be a fight in the water or something?"

"The fight is what we're trying to avoid. Look, Tommy, you live in a small town on that side of the river. You're the governor of the town, and we'll also make you general of an army. Your name will be Julius."

"I'm not taking that name. That's a half-girl and half-boy's name or something."

"Okay, then you'll be known as Caesar the Great."

"That's better. I like that name."

Bobby started to really get into the storytelling. He was talking with his hands like Mom's Italian neighbor friends back in Cincy. He fluffed up the pillow, trying to make the little but very important river bigger. "I live on this side of the Rubicon, and my name is Pompey," he said.

"Why do we have to have such queer names?" I asked.

"Because this is a true story of people who lived back before Jesus was born. We're using their real names."

"Why didn't you say so in the beginning? Okay, go ahead."

"I live, unlike you, in the biggest city in the world—Rome."

"My teacher said that New York City is the biggest city."

"How stupid are you? There was no New York City back then. This story takes place some two thousand years ago."

"How am I supposed to know that?" I asked. "You should have told me that at the beginning too."

I knew Ronny was smiling. He was gulping, and his ears were moving. He bent forward, his papers pressed between his elbow and leg, with his chin in his hand. He was looking down, petting Mildred. "Please tell me you're not giving up on the story," he said.

"No way," Bobby replied. "He needs to understand the reason why I'm telling the story. Now, Tommy, I'm the leader, the king if you will, over this vast Roman Empire."

"What is *vast*?" I asked.

"It means big, large," he said.

"Why do you get to be king?"

"Because I'm in Rome on this side of the Rubicon, and I'm also bigger than you. Now, are you going to shut up long enough for me to tell the story?"

"Yeah, go on."

"Caesar, you are my most important field general."

"I thought my name was Caesar the Great."

"Listen, you moron, your full name is Thomas Brooks, but people call you Tommy, don't they?"

"Yes."

"It's the same thing," he said.

"I know, but if I were a general and had an army, I'd want to be called Tommy the Great."

Ronny, still smiling, looked over at Bobby and asked, "You give up yet?"

Bobby leaned back and put his hands behind his head. "I give."

"What do you mean, you give?" I said. "We're not wrestling. You can't 'give' on telling a story."

"Oh, believe me, Tommy, he's been wrestling," Ronny said.

"I don't care," I said. "It's a dumb story anyway. Just tell me, Bobby, did Caesar ever cross the Rubicon?"

"Yes, he did, and this is where he said the famous words, 'The die is cast.'"

"So did Caesar die or did you, the other guy, die and get thrown into the Rubicon?"

"No, Tommy," Ronny said. "In this case, die means dice, not to die as in dead."

"You're kidding me, right? Die can't mean two different things like that, can it?"

"Yes," Bobby said, "once Caesar had taken his army across the Rubicon, he had rolled the dice. He took the chance and had to either conquer Rome or die."

"You told me this long story just to let me know that if I cross the Rubicon, one of us will die?" I asked.

"No, not one of us," Bobby said. "You will die, as in dead!"

"So Caesar the Great died and was *casted* into the river?" I asked.

"I didn't say anything about anyone being cast into the river," Bobby said. "There's no such word as *casted,* and how do you even know what cast means?"

"I learned that word fishing with Uncle Lou," I said. "He let me cast with his rod and reel in the Ohio. See, you don't know everything, Bobby."

"I know there's another meaning for the word *cast*," he said.

"Ronny, does cast mean two things too?" I asked.

"Yes," he said.

"Hopefully, the molds were *casted* into the river after you and Crazy were made," Bobby said.

It seemed as though Ronny kept a count, a certain number of times that he would let Bobby get away with calling names and hitting him. Then Bobby's head would hit the wall, he'd fall down the stairs, or he'd step on a nail. Something would happen where it looked like it could have been an accident or Ronny's fault. Ronny was always ready with the saying, "Bobby, you're as clumsy as an ox!"

I think Mom knew that it was probably Ronny's doings. I'd heard her tell Bobby more than once that he'd better be careful. Whenever Bobby had said or done something wrong to Ronny, her saying was, "You know he's just biding his time." I didn't know that *biding* meant waiting for the right time, but I knew Ronny wouldn't forget.

"One last time, do I—Caesar the Great—die, or do I kick your butt, Pump-pee?"

"The name is Pompey, you little squirt," Bobby said, "and the ending doesn't matter now that you truly understand the consequences of crossing the Rubicon."

"Surely you're going to tell him the real ending to this supposedly true story," Ronny said. "Tommy, that's not the way it ended in my world history class."

Bobby jabbed his left elbow into my chest, pushing me back into the seat. At the same time he threw a fast hard right that crushed Ronny's right shoulder.

Ronny looked over as if it hadn't hurt. "What are you doing?" he asked. "We don't have room to play tag in the car. You still lose. Why don't you admit that you picked the wrong side of the river and that your great example backfired?"

"Ronny, did I win? Is that why Bobby named me 'the Great'?"

"That's right," Ronny said. "Now you get to control the boundaries. Here's the Rubicon." He had reached over, snatched the pillow, and stuck it behind his back.

Bobby was lying across me, grabbing and swinging. Ronny was smiling, blocking and pushing Bobby off.

Dad slowed down and pulled off the road. He got out and pulled the back of his seat forward. While he was still standing outside the car, he reached in with his left arm and started swinging. He managed to land a few hard ones on Ronny's face and head, but Ronny kept smiling and blocking the best he could.

Bobby was back in his seat. Mom had reached over, pulled on Dad's arm, and told him to stop and get back in the car.

"Hey, that's not fair," I said. "Bobby started it!"

"Keep quiet and mind your own business back there," Dad said.

"It is my business. I won the fight in Rome, and I control the Rubicon, so the pillow is now mine. Right, Ronny?"

Ronny didn't answer. His face was down in his arms, which were folded across his legs.

Bobby was already lying back, eyes closed, with his head on the pillow.

"Why don't you ever hit Bobby?" I asked. "You always hit Ronny. It's because Bobby's your pet, right?"

"Tommy, you be still," Mom said. "Sit back and close your eyes for a while. We're going to be in Tennessee before long. Then we'll stop, get something to drink, and eat our baloney sandwiches."

"No, you should make him stop and beat Bobby too," I insisted.

"I'm going to stop and beat you if you don't shut up!" Dad said.

"I don't care!"

"You better start caring," Dad said.

Ronny slid his hand over, patted my knee, and whispered, "That's enough, Tommy."

The next thing I remember hearing was Mom telling me, "Wake up. It's time to eat. We're in Jellico, Tennessee."

"It must be jelly, 'cause jam don't shake like that!" Ronny yelled at a couple of girls walking down the street.

Dad reached around and popped him on the side of the head. "Never yell at people from my car, and never say things like that to young ladies."

I thought it was really something that Ronny was smart enough to make up a saying like that in a town with that name.

Dad looked at Mom and added, "From what I could see, it looked like tasty jam to me."

Mom got mad. "That was not a nice thing to say in front of the kids!" Those were the last words she spoke all the way through Tennessee.

I asked Ronny to explain Dad's tasty jam saying.

He whispered, "It meant he liked the same thing I did, their butts."

I wondered if Mom was supposed to hit Dad in the head for what he said. It was years later before I found out that Ronny's saying was from a song written before I was even born. It was still pretty smart of him to think of the words that fast.

It seemed like we were in Tennessee forever. Mom wasn't saying anything, but it was easy getting Ronny and Bobby talking again.

All I had to do was ask. "Bobby, what do you think your used-to-be girlfriend is doing right now?"

"She's Spike's chick by now," Ronny said.

"Shut up, you crazy little hood!" Bobby said.

Spike Sweeny was Bobby's best friend, but Mom's saying was "Sweeny's sweet on Barbie too."

"Bobby, Mom's usually right, and she said that Sweeny had the eye for her," I said.

"She's probably getting familiar with the big Spike tonight," Ronny piped up.

"Watch your play on words with that big mouth of yours, you punk," Bobby said.

"Oh, I'm sorry," Ronny said. "I can see where one might think getting familiar with the big Spike could be making reference to Sweeny's weenie."

"Knock off that kind of talk back there!" Dad yelled.

Wow, that was the first time he had corrected Ronny without swinging. Ronny should have written that down.

"You really think that Spike or other guys aren't going to be trying to play 'kissy face' with her now that you're gone?" Ronny asked.

"Spike's a real friend," Bobby said, "something you've never had. He's going to watch out for her for me."

"So tell us just exactly what your great friend is going to do," Ronny said.

"He's going to meet her and walk her to her classes whenever he can."

"Is he allowed to carry her books and walk her home from school like you did?" Ronny asked. "Is he also going to take her to the school dances but not dance with her or let her dance with anyone else?"

"The answer is yes to your dumb questions," Bobby said. "She's on the dance committee, and that's the only reason she goes to the school dances. He has to walk her home from school to keep guys like you from bothering her. Tell me why you're writing down everything I say, you crazy nut."

"I'm going to read this back to you in a few weeks. If you still believe this garbage, we'll let Tommy decide who's crazy. Even he's smart enough to figure this out. Tommy, don't you think Barbara is already wearing Spike's letterman sweater?"

I could see tears filling up in Bobby's eyes. "No way will Barbara ever wear Spike's sweater," I said. "She loves Bobby too much. I've seen her kiss him right on his lips with her eyes closed."

"What does that have to do with a hill of beans?" Ronny asked.

"It has nothing to do with beans, but Mom said in order to love someone, you must get to know them."

"So?" Ronny said.

"So she must really know Bobby if she can find his lips with her eyes closed," I said.

"You still think he's smart enough to decide who's what?" Bobby asked.

"Looking doubtful," Ronny said. He smiled big and went back to writing.

The trip had been great so far. I couldn't believe that maybe I was going to get to decide something between those two. Dad got to decide a lot of things. He got to decide to take a nap and rest his eyes while we were in the Stuckey store. He also decided to let Mom have money to buy a pecan roll. We all got a bite, except for Ronny. After Dad and Bobby took their big bites, there was only a little left. I tried to give Ronny his part, but he said that I could have the rest. It was really good, and I know he wanted some.

Dad also decided to keep on driving through the night, instead of stopping at a motel like Mom and I wanted to. Mom asked him to gas up back at the nice, new Stuckey's, but he decided he would wait.

A couple hours later the car started cutting out. Dad hit the heel of his hand on the top of the steering wheel. "Damn it, damn it, damn it!" He rocked backward and forward in his seat, trying to keep the car rolling as he pulled off the road.

Mom woke up. "Why are you cursing, and where are we?"

"We're on some back road out of Macon, and we're out of gas," he said.

Mom started nervously rubbing her hands together. "I asked you to fill up."

"Don't start, Irene. I didn't know every gas station in the state would be closed during the night. I kept thinking there would be a truck stop around the next bend. Let's all go to sleep for a couple hours. When the sun comes up, we'll be able to see where we are, get gas, and get back on the road."

The sun had already been up for an hour before the wind from a fast passing truck shook the car and woke us up. We could see Dad and Bobby going down the road holding their thumbs out as they walked. An hour was a long time sitting still and waiting in that car. It was getting hot, even with the windows down. Finally, a truck stopped on the other side of the road, and Bobby and Dad got out with an old gallon apple cider jar full of gas.

Dad poured most of the gas into the tank and told Bobby to raise the hood. Ronny had gotten out, but Dad told him to get back in the car, that he didn't need his help. Ronny got back in, crossed over me, and took Mildred out Mom's door. Keeping Mildred close to the car, he walked her around the back, up to the driver's side. He was smiling big as he hid behind the open door and let Mildred do her duty. Ronny and Mildred jumped back in the car beside me.

"Ronny, you're going to get it," I said.

"I didn't do anything," he said. "When Mildred has to go, she has to go. It's the call of nature."

"Bobby, get in and turn the car on while I put a little gas in the carb," Dad said. "Make sure you let go of the key the second the engine turns over so you don't ruin the starter."

It cranked up on the third try.

Mom clapped her hands and said, "Praise the Lord!"

The car made a weird scraping, whining sound.

"Let go of the key!" Dad yelled. He dropped the jar, ran back, and pulled Bobby out from behind the wheel by his arm. "Get out! Do you think you can close the hood without breaking the latch? Grab Della's jar. We have to take it back."

After he put the hood down, Bobby got in and held the jar on his lap.

"Who is Della, and what is that smell?" Mom asked.

"It's stinky Millie!" yelled my little sister.

"No, it's not," I said. "It's Bobby." I could see that the dog crap had squished up on the side of his gym shoe. He should have looked instead of reaching to check the bottom of his shoes.

"Shit, oh shit!" Bobby yelled. "Stop the car. I've got dog crap all over me."

Dad pulled over, and Bobby got out. Mom gave him the cartoon section from the newspaper Dad had gotten at Stuckey's. Ronny hadn't said one word this whole time. Bobby kept wiping and wiping.

"That's good enough," Dad said. "Get in. You can wash up at Della's."

Bobby got back in with his shoe in his hand.

"It only got on your left shoe," I said.

"Isn't that enough, you little ass?" he said as he put me in a headlock.

He started rubbing my face with his paper-wiped "doo-doo" hand that smelled really bad. "Who took the dog out, you or your crazy partner?" he asked.

Ronny still hadn't said a thing.

Bobby continued to rub my face.

"Stop it!" I said. "You're going to make me throw up. How do you know it was Mildred that did it and not some other dog?"

"Let's see, a fresh pile of dog crap on the side of the road. It was obviously close to our car. We're parked out in the middle of nowhere. Only one dog within . . . Never mind. I wonder why I even bother."

"I wonder, too, why you do what you do," Ronny chimed in.

"Dad, how much longer?" Bobby asked.

"Only a few more miles, and we'll be at Della's," Dad replied.

"No, I mean putting up with him like this."

"Tommy, behave back there and scoot over some," Dad said.

"Bobby's talking about Ronny, not me. I didn't say anything, and I can't move over anymore, if Ronny and Mildred don't move. If Bobby would give up the fake Rubicon pillow, we'd have lots of room."

"Who is Della?" Mom asked again. "Some woman standing with a jar of gas on the side of the road or something?"

"Oh no," Bobby answered. "She owns Della's Diner, and she's nice looking too. Mom, wait till you hear her accent. It killed me when she said, 'Well, it sure is nice to meet you, Bob-by,' in that soft Southern voice. She managed to draw Bobby out into a three-syllable word. No one has ever said my name like that."

"It looks like her and her husband converted their house into a diner," Dad said.

"It's jacked," Bobby said. "It sits up off the ground about three feet on cinder blocks. The jar of gas was under the side of the house. I know she's not taken. She's back on the market."

"What makes you think that?" Dad asked.

"Because, when she pulled the jar out and wiped off the sand and cobwebs, she said, 'It's a wonder my used-to-be husband didn't drink this too.'"

Bobby hadn't been that perky for quite some time. He kept on talking, and Ronny kept on writing.

"What does she look like?" I asked.

"She looks like a thirty-six, twenty-four, thirty-six swinging in a tight, pure white skirt. It ends a couple inches just above the knees. Her gorgeous, suntanned legs run up and up into her—"

"That's enough description," Mom said.

Bobby kept on. "But I haven't gotten to the snug blouse with the top two buttons open and her name badge that sticks way out because of her voluptuous—"

"And that she's way too old for you," Dad said.

"She's not old," Bobby said.

"The diner wasn't even open yet," Dad said. "Who do you think owned the two little kids running around?"

"The lady sitting out on the front porch," Bobby answered.

"No, the kids called her Granny," Dad said. "That was Della's mother on the breezeway."

"Dad, what's a breezeway?" I asked.

"Well, it's kind of like a screened-in porch in the South."

"Why do they screen in the porch?"

"So the mosquitoes don't carry you off," he said.

"Mosquitoes get that big down here?"

"Yes, and they're even bigger in Florida."

"Shut up and listen to how Bobby's already forgetting his Cincinnati girl," Ronny whispered in my ear.

The heck with Bobby's Barbie back in Cincy, I thought. I was worried about those big-ass mosquitoes waiting for me in Florida.

"Listening to you two carrying on about this Della makes me feel like I should know her," Mom said.

There it was up on the left-hand side of the road, a blinking sign that said, *Della's Diner's Open*. Printed below it was *Address Truckers Home Away from Home!*

Dad pulled up and parked next to a giant truck. I counted; it had eighteen really big wheels.

"Bobby, run that jar in, and tell her thanks," Dad said.

"Jim, we're all hungry," Mom said. "There's only one baloney sandwich left, and it doesn't smell good."

"Okay, let's go in and check out the prices on the menu."

"If it's too much, we'll just get a drink and stop at a grocery store on down the road," Mom said.

"There are a few truckers in there eating, so the food should be good," Dad said.

"Ronny, hurry and get out," I said. "Let's go eat. Tell me, why do they get to use words for addresses down here, but we had to use numbers?"

"That's not the real address. It's just a saying."

"Oh no, they got 'em down here too?" I asked.

"Yeah, they probably have a lot more and a lot different."

Dad got out, pulled up the back of the seat, and said, "Come on, get out."

The second Ronny's left foot hit the ground, Dad grabbed him by the back of the neck. "Don't let me have any trouble with you in here, and don't talk if you can't talk right."

I put my arm around Ronny's waist and pulled him away. "Come on, let's race to the door."

Dad let him go, but Ronny didn't run fast. It was like what Dad had said took the spirit or the "want to" right out of him.

That was the first time I saw, felt, and really understood one of Mom's sayings. When Dad would overcorrect, preach, or beat one of us, Mom would say, "Jim, stop now. Don't break his spirit!"

Spirit nothing—we were worried about him breaking bones. That morning on a back road out of Macon, I felt the sorrow of a broken spirit, and it wasn't even mine. I wondered if the broken spirit and the broken heart that Mom talked about were one and the same. If not, I'm sure Ronny had both that day.

Kissy Face

Verse
The teacher's giving you Shakespeare, art, and history
So you better keep your eyes on the book
Instead of my girl in row three
You can get caught passing her a note
To get an answer you can only hope
You can get caught carrying her books
Walking her to class giving her looks
Buy her lunch, do her homework
Sharpen her pencil like a big dumb jerk, but

Chorus
Don't let me catch you playing kissy face with my girl
Don't let me catch you playing kissy face with my girl
Don't let me catch you playing kissy face with my girl
Don't let me catch you playing kissy face

Verse
The word is out for all you cats that really think you're cool
Don't try to score on my number one squeeze
Or you might not make it through school
You can go ahead and walk her home
Buy her a soda, call her on the phone
You can get caught with matching shirts
On Sadie Hawkins Day and Girls Reverse
After the game you can ask her to dance
In your mind you can think it's romance, but

Chorus Repeat

Chapter 6
The Blue Plate Special

Bobby was already holding the screen door open leading into the breezeway. That was my first new Southern word. I thought it was funny. I had heard of a fairway, a highway, a hideaway, but never a breezeway. Of course I never figured out why we park in driveways and drive on parkways. The word *Enter,* with an *E* was painted just above the door. It had been painted freehand with white lettering right on the breezeway screen.

Most of the screen was old looking. It was loose and wavy, with a few big holes—probably from those bigheaded mosquitoes. Just inside to the left were three rocking chairs in a row. Each had a small barrel turned upside down to serve as an end table. An old, repainted red, double-seated swing couch was centered just behind the rockers. A new red-and-white Coke machine with the shiny lever was against the wall. It stood just to the right of an unfinished archway, which led into the remodeled living room turned diner.

As Ronny started up the three old, outside wooden steps, Bobby pulled the door open as far as he could, stood back, and let the screen door fly. His timing was perfect for injury. The one thing that wasn't old was the heavy-duty overloaded spring that swung the door closed. The screen door's hardwood frame hit Ronny on the side of his head and the back of his right shoulder. His papers went flying—some inside, some outside. Here I thought Bobby was holding the door to make this Della think he was nice, older, and cooler.

Mom walked in holding her purse close, tight, and high under her left breast. She always looked as if she was protecting a bag of money that I knew she didn't have. I'd seen inside Mom's purse before but never without her doing the opening. I could run and get the purse for her from one of her many hiding places, but I was never allowed to open it. "Not even your father gets in my purse," she would say. That was true, but I never figured out why. She had nothing but a bright red tube of lipstick, a compact with a cracked mirror, a hanky, and a small coin purse with some loose change—sometimes.

She did have a Social Security card she didn't need because she never worked outside the home. She said that was Dad's fault for making her have all us kids. She claimed he was also jealous, and that he had a "stay-at-home-and-work-me-like-a-slave" belief. She just may have been right, again.

"Jim, take a look at how nice she has this setup. Customers can sit out here, rock in the fresh country air, have a cold drink, talk, and enjoy the breeze."

Breeze? There was no breeze. I hadn't felt air blowing since we left Cincinnati—that is, unless Dad was going fifty miles per hour with the windows down. Ronny picked up his loose papers from off the floor, along with his stapled-together finished writings. He got up off his knees, never looked up, and walked out the door.

"Don't wake your sister, and leave those papers in the car," Dad said.

I knew Ronny had to be hungry, but I didn't think he was coming back in. As we passed through the arch, I heard phonics like I'd never heard before.

"Now that's a real Southern drawl," Dad said.

I know that my two-times fourth-grade teacher, Mrs. Flanagan, would have passed out.

"Welcome to Della's. Y'all come on in and grab a spot. Y'all must be hot and tired from all that driving."

Bobby stood there like a goof, staring with smiling eyes, mouth open, holding the empty cider bottle with his smelly hand. His tight Levi's were always two inches short of touching his tennis shoes.

"It was Bob-by, wasn't it?" she asked.

He didn't—or couldn't—answer right away.

"What's wrong? The cat got your tongue?"

That was it, my first Southern saying. At least the first one heard in the South. I had no idea what a cat had to do with Bobby's tongue. But the way the words rolled off of her tongue was really something. She did have prettier legs than any of the high school girl tennis players. I believe Della's breasts were the reason Bobby couldn't talk, not a cat. While she asked him his name, making sure it was "Bob-by," she bent forward cleaning off a table. With every wipe of the towel, her breasts shook.

I asked Bobby why he didn't answer her.

He said he was "busy praying for a fallout."

"She's just darling and has a really nice back porch," Mom said to Dad.

"Mom, it's called a breezeway in the South, and if it were a porch, it would be the front, not the back," I said.

She laughed and said, "Oh, you're right, Tommy. We came in the front, didn't we?"

"Yeah, but I'd like to see Della's back porch too," Dad said.

That's all he said, and Mom wasn't talking to him again.

In the middle of the room was a round table stacked with blue plastic plates a foot high. The guy who made these might have been smarter than the guy who cleaned and resold the used newspaper. The plates were divided into sections so the different foods couldn't touch each other. What a great idea! No spinach or peas touching the mashed potatoes, and no fruit like applesauce getting on the meat. Taped to the edge of the table was another handwritten sign.

"Mom, read that sign," I said. "Does it read right to you?"

"You haven't lived till you did the blue plate special," she read.

"That should be 'had,' not 'did.' Right, Mom?"

"That's very good, Tommy, that you were able to pick that up."

Bobby started clapping with two fingers, squinting up his face. "Bravo, bravo! Did you learn that your first year or second year in the—"

Mom stuck a fork to Bobby's arm. I didn't care what he said, because I was feeling pretty smart and couldn't wait to point it out to Della.

Della walked over with her pen and pad. "Y'all have enough time to look at the menu?" she asked, drawing the word *menu* out to sound like *menyoo*. "Do you have any questions I can answer for ya?"

"Yes, I want the blue plate special," I said.

"Honey, it's too early for the special. We don't serve the blue plate till afternoon. You wouldn't like today's special anyway, Tom-my."

"How do you know I won't like it, and how did you know my name?"

"I heard your momma call you that. It is Tom-my, right?"

"Yes, but you say it a little different."

"Like how ya mean?"

"Well, you draw out your vowels, or your phonic sounds are longer, I think."

"Why, Tommy, you're smart in English, ain't ya?" she asked. "You think I talk funny, don't ya?" She winked at Dad, who was already in enough trouble.

"No, yeah, maybe—but Bobby really likes the way you talk. You're all he's talked about since we got the car started, except for when he stepped in some strange dog shit."

"Tommy!" Mom exclaimed. "Never say that word, and never, ever say something like that in an eating establishment."

"But—"

"But nothing, and don't try to blame it on Ronny or anyone else."

"Mom, it was Bobby who said it first, when he got it all over his hand from off his shoe."

"Tommy, that's enough," Mom said.

I thought I'd better wait for another time to ask Bobby what another word was for establishment. I'd never seen a face get so red so fast.

"Now Bob-by, don't you be blushing. You know what you wanna order yet?"

"No, ma'am," he said.

"Don't you go ma'aming me. We're not that far different in age. Okay, Tommy, back to why you wouldn't like the special. Do you like ham hocks, collard greens, and okra with some corn bread and buttermilk?"

"No, I don't think so, but does the hamburger look like the picture on the wall with the French fries?"

"It sure does, Tommy, but it's still breakfast time. You know what? I do have one burger patty made up back there, and I'll cook it up just for you."

"Can you cut it in two, so I can take half to Ronny?" I asked.

"Who and where is Ronny?"

"He's one of my other brothers."

"He's out in the car, mad," Bobby said.

"He's not mad, he's hurt," I said.

"That door didn't hurt that bad," Bobby said.

"I mean he's hurt down inside," I explained, "like down in his heart again, and it could be broken this time. It doesn't feel good, Bobby."

"Well," Della said, "I'm mad and hurt that Ronny didn't come in and eat at Della's. You all figure out what you want. I'll be right back." She disappeared through the arch.

Mom and Bobby decided on pancakes. Dad was getting bacon and eggs, sunny side up, with a side of grits, whatever that was. Within minutes, Della reappeared from under the arch holding my little sister's hand. She had her other arm wrapped around, under, and through Ronny's arm, as if they were close friends.

I jumped up and asked Della, "Can we sit at that table on the other side of those two men, or is that for truckers only?"

"Why, sure ya can." She took my little sister over to eat at the table with her mom and her two little kids.

Ronny and I sat at a little table where there was only room for two. It was right under the writing on the wall. *Restroom down the Hall-Left / Kitchen-Right / Stay out of Kitchen.* A wavy arrow above the word *restroom* pointed the way. On the other wall was a square, window-like opening into the kitchen. Across the top of it was a wire. Hanging on it were the same kind of clothespins that Mom had on her basement lines.

"Let's get moving back there," Della yelled. "New order up."

At the same time she went up on her right tippy toes with a little air kick from the left leg. She leaned forward, reached high with her left arm, and clipped the ticket on the line. Her white tight skirt got shorter, and her legs got longer.

The two truckers next to us were smiling. The younger one had a greasy baseball hat turned upside down on the table next to his plate. "Man, look at that Coke-bottle figure," he said. "I'd sure like to order some of that."

"She's way too classy for you," said the older coffee-drinking, chain-smoking trucker from across the table. After a cough and a hack, he continued, "You best stick to what's written on the menu."

"Why?" asked the young greasy-hat trucker, who was also wearing a bad-looking Roy Rogers type cowboy shirt.

"I heard she sent her drunken old man packing, guitar and all," said the older trucker.

"Then the timing's just right for pickin'," he replied.

"Still, I'd hate to see the price you'd have to pay if he ever caught you with Della. Best you only keep to looking," said the old trucker, as he blew a perfect round smoke ring to the ceiling.

The young trucker stood up and pushed his hair back. He popped his hat on his head, put a toothpick in his mouth, and started rolling it from side to side. His eyes were rolling too. They were rolling up and down Della, as she was hanging up over the ledge of the order window. She got down with a little jump and slowly walked back toward the truckers' table.

"Hey, Della, I have a full load to pull down to Orleans, so I gotta get back on the road. Whaddya say that when I come back through, you and I put in a little 'overtime' together?"

"Only in your dreams, cowboy. I just got rid of one like you." She patted him on the cheek as she sidestepped slow and easy between him and the table. "On the way back, make sure ya still stop in and grab ya a bite."

He smiled with a continuous nodding of the chin and a breathy, "That's what I'm talking about . . ."

She looked back over her shoulder, smiled with a stretched-out arm, bent down wrist, and pointed finger, and said, "A bite of food, you little devil."

Ronny had his papers out on the table even though Dad had told him to leave them in the car. He was listening, looking, and writing all this time, not saying a word. Bobby had gotten up to go to the restroom, hopefully to wash his hands. I know Ronny didn't see him, but he must have felt him. His timing was even better than Bobby's release of the screen door.

Ronny was leaning forward with his weight on the front legs of an old, bent, wooden chair. The back legs were an inch off the floor. Just as Bobby cut past our table, Ronny pivoted off the left front leg and twisted the chair, catching Bobby's foot with its back right leg. Bobby tripped, fell, and bounced into the hallway with a bloody lip. Ronny was smiling, and I was laughing. Boy, did Bobby look funny tumbling across the floor, trying to save himself. When one of us got hurt and looked stupid doing it, the rest of us laughed. Mom said she had some "very troubled children."

"Bobby, you need to be careful," Ronny said. "When was the last time you talked to your feet?"

Bobby didn't answer but kept right on going down the hall into the restroom. I was sure he hoped Della hadn't seen what happened and he didn't want Della to see his bloody lip, but I really needed to hear his answer. I had never talked to my feet, didn't know I was supposed to, and didn't know anyone who did. It was just that the way Ronny asked the question made it sound like a good idea.

Dad stormed over to me. "What happened?" he demanded.

"Ronny moved his chair, and Bobby tripped," I explained.

Dad pushed Ronny's head down, holding his forehead flat against the table. "I told you that I didn't want any trouble out of you!"

Ronny remained still and quiet, his arms hanging limp at his sides.

Dad leaned down to Ronny's ear. "Can you not hear me in there? I told you to leave these papers in the car." Dad snatched up all of Ronny's papers and wadded them up as he walked down to the restroom.

"Hey, Dad, those belong to Ronny! You don't even know what he's writing because you've never asked to . . ."

I couldn't complete the sentence as the air left my body. Ronny's head was still down, but his arms weren't hanging limp anymore. He had reached under the table and pulled my leg straight. He dug his nails into my skin just above my ankle. He didn't lift, only twisted his head so I could see his eyes.

"Ronny, Dad didn't hear me. I forgot. He was halfway down the hall. No way did he hear me."

Ronny slowly pulled his head up and sat back in his chair. He looked at me with a cold, blank stare. "Tommy, if because of you he asks, or if I find out that he read my stuff . . ." He didn't blink or move.

A few seconds later they came back into the diner. Dad was empty-handed and Bobby was holding a piece of wet toilet paper to his lip. As they walked past us, Dad said, "Keep quiet, stay in your seats, and eat your burger."

Bobby was so mad, he didn't even look our way. It was his own fault. In the end Ronny would win. He knew that.

No sooner had Dad and Bobby sat back down at their table than Mom got up and came over. She came up behind me and put her hands on my shoulders. "I'm sure that was an accident," she said. "Is everything okay at this table?"

"Everything is just wonderful," Ronny said.

"Tommy, I want you to be a sweet boy. I saw you laughing at Bobby. I guess it did look funny to you, but Tommy, today is a new day, and I want you to 'turn over a new leaf.'"

Laughing? By then I was trying to keep tears from running down my face at the same time blood was running over my sock.

She slowly rubbed my cheek with the back of her hand a few times, gave Ronny a smile, and went back to her table.

"Why do I have to figure out what she means by turning over a new leaf?" I asked. "I heard you smiling. Why don't you have to find a new leaf to turn over?"

"Maybe I don't have as many things to change as you."

"So it means I have to change? Change what? Why didn't she just tell me what to change? Is this a Southern saying?"

"No, it's an everywhere saying. Mom's talking in general about your feelings and actions toward others and things. It's not about Bobby."

"That's good, because when I think of him falling and trying to catch himself, I almost wet my pants. What leaf do you think Mom wants me to turn over?"

"It's not a real turning of a leaf. It means the same as to turn the page, erase the blackboard, and start with a clean slate."

"You're kidding me, right?"

"Look, Tommy, we're moving to Florida. It means new schools, new teachers, new friends, and a new church—that is, if one of those tent preachers can convince Dad."

"Convince him to what," I asked.

"Convince him to repent and be baptized by fire and water. Do you understand now what Mom is trying to tell you?"

"Not at all. I know we're moving and that all those things are going to be new. I'm not that dumb!"

"Mom is saying that you now have a chance at a fresh new start. She's saying that you're a poor student. The teachers can hardly put up with your dumb questions. Your school friends are 'not too smart.'"

"Yeah, I wonder sometimes why I don't talk or play with the smarter kids."

"You don't because birds of a feather flock together."

"Birds of a feather?" I asked.

"Yes, it's a saying, meaning in this case that 'not too smart' flocks with 'not too smart.'"

"You're the one who's not too smart. I was right here. Mom didn't say any of that stuff about me! Dad will also be not too smart if he repents, the fire starts, and if there's not enough water."

"Tommy, you really are not too smart."

That soft Southern voice came up behind me. "Tommy, how's that hamburger? You like it?"

"It's the best hamburger I've ever had, but please don't tell my mom."

"Why not?"

"I don't want her to feel bad."

"Why not? You made your brother Bobby feel bad."

"I didn't make him fall," I said. "I only laughed. He went down hard. Did you see him fall?"

"Tommy, not too much is said or done in this diner that I don't hear or see. So what ya say?"

"So what ya say, what?" I asked.

"So what ya say you go tell Bobby you're sorry?"

"Sorry for what, laughing?"

Della turned my chair around a little and closed in on me. Boy, did she smell good. "Look deep into my eyes," she said.

I did, and they were not only pretty but as blue as the sky.

"Tommy, as human beings, what lies behind us or lies before us is determined by what lies inside of us." She turned and started to walk away.

I felt sorry for Ronny. He didn't get to smell her or look deep into her eyes. I could hear him mumbling to himself over and over what Della had said to me.

"Miss Della!" I called her that because I had heard some of the truckers calling her that way. "Is that a Southern saying?"

"No, Mr. Tommy." She chuckled. "That was advice given by a wise Southern gentleman to his hard-headed daughter about a man she thought loved her."

"My mom knows all the Bible stories and a lot about love. She even knows the definition. Come on, let's go over and ask my mom."

"My help just got here. Let me turn some tables over, and I'll be right there."

I walked over to the table and stood there holding onto the back of Mom's chair.

"Did you eat all of your burger?" she asked.

"Yeah, and it was really good and big. I ate half, and Ronny is still eating his half."

"What was Della telling you?"

"Something about what lies ahead or lies behind comes from what lies inside."

"Did she think you were lying to her about something?"

"No, I think she was talking about something lying down in front or in back of somebody. Both the *lie* words sound the same. I don't know how she was spelling it, so I don't know which one she was using."

"They're both spelled the same, you pea-brain," Bobby said, as some blood ran off his bottom lip.

"He's lying. Right, Mom?"

"No, he's not lying."

"I'm never going to get through school, and I'm not lying either!"

I turned around, and my face was right in Della's stomach. She put her left hand on my back, her right hand on my left cheek, and pulled my head in tight to her. "This one here is a lot smarter than he knows," she said. "If he was only a little older, we'd be courting."

Facing up looking between her breasts, I could see her joking smile as she looked toward Bobby across the table. "It's Bobby who likes you," I said.

"Dad, I'm going to kill him!"

She started rocking me from my one foot to the other, holding me tighter and closer. Ronny came over and leaned against the wall, watching and listening.

I thought that this had to be a bosom hug. Mom used to try to explain what *bosom* meant when reading the Bible stories to us. Ronny would say if the robe was open you could see their "attics." Mom would say the bosom was below the attics. I found out from Bobby that Ronny was right. I guessed that Mom just didn't want us thinking of attics during Bible reading. Mom did fall for it when I told her to look down her shirt and spell the word *attic*.

"*A-T-T-I-C*," she said. It took a few seconds before she caught on and tried not to laugh. "Oh, good Lord, what are you learning out there on the streets?"

"Nothing. I learned that from Ronny."

She told me not to ask Dad to do that; he might not think it was funny. I never did because Mom said not to.

"Now Bob-by, when Tommy gets older, he'll see," Della said.

"He's not going to live to get older to see anything!" Bobby said.

"Bob-by, he'll learn why boys and girls like you and I could or would like one another. Don't go being all upset at him. Someday Tom-my will have a girlfriend, and then he'll understand."

"I don't want a girlfriend like Bobby's because she already has another boyfriend."

"She does, does she?"

"Yeah, and Ronny said that she's already getting familiar with the big Spike." "Tommy!"

"What, Mom?" Della said.

"Sorry, Della. Spike is the boy's name."

"Relax now, Momma, I heard. That's what Tommy just said, and that Spike was big too."

Della turned me loose, lightly running her fingers across the top of my head. "Bob-by, when you get to Florida, get ya another one. There's lots of girls out there just like me that would *love* to be your girlfriend." She started clearing our table.

Dad got up and said he was going out to walk around and stretch his legs. I think he just wanted to check out Della's back porch.

Once Dad was out of hearing range, Bobby started talking. "It's not that easy to find someone who looks good, feels good, and smells—"

"Bob-by, her looking nice and feeling good is not all it's about," Della said, in a matter-of-fact voice.

"Della's right," Mom said. "We talked about love on the way here."

"I know we did, but it's hard."

"Bob-by, was the feeling of love only there when she wanted something?" Della asked.

Bobby wasn't answering, so I answered for him. "Hard to tell. He was always doing something for her."

Bobby gave me the hate look.

"Was it a surface, physical-only feeling on her part?"

"He was physical," I said, "always trying to hug her and hold her hand, even when others were around. I don't think she liked it much."

Bobby said nothing. He had his head down, his eyes staring up hard at me.

"Did she still care for you during the times you had nothing to give?" Della asked.

"The big Spike is giving it to her now."

"Oh, good Lord, Tommy!" Mom yelled.

Ronny was still leaning against the wall, but at least I heard him smile.

"Ronny was the one that said Spike gave her his letterman sweater," I said, defending myself. "Now Spike has to take the time to walk her to class and carry her books."

"Bob-by, make sure your next girl's love is coming from the inside out."

"It's a good thing their father's not here right now," Mom said. "We could never talk so open like this."

"Ronny, you okay?" Della asked. "Can I get you another soda or something else to eat?"

"No, but can I use the restroom before we go?"

"You sure may. You go right ahead, young man."

Ronny had no sooner disappeared down the hallway than Dad came through the breezeway and went straight back to the restroom. That was another thing that bothered me. The changing of the toilet room signs to *bath* or *restroom*, even with no tub, seat, or bed in them. It didn't make sense. When I asked my mom why, she said it was because they were nicer words.

So we also had words that really meant something else and stood for something they weren't. The only thing in the restroom down that hall was a toilet and a tall wire wastebasket. Oh yeah, and an old, spotted, cloudy mirror hanging a foot too high over the sink. I couldn't see if I had boogers in my nose without jumping.

It was only a few minutes before the ringing sound of the bouncing iron basket came down the hall. Ronny came out from the hallway head down, holding the back of his neck, and went straight out the front. From across the diner we could hear Dad drag the basket back into the restroom and slam the door. Dad came out, picked up my little sister, and pointed at Mom. "You have ten minutes to be in the car. It's time to go."

As soon as Mom heard Dad's extra-heavy walking on the breezeway's wooden floorboards, she jumped up from her chair. She left the food money on the table. She must have counted it a dozen times. "Come on, Tommy. Let's not keep your father waiting. Della, that was a lovely breakfast. We enjoyed it very much. Bobby, you can bring that pop with you. Let's go now." Mom walked quickly between and around tables saying, "Excuse me, pardon me," to people she hadn't even bothered.

Bobby stood up and stayed behind the table, slowly sipping on his straw, trying to look tough.

Della bent over to me and whispered, "You behave now, Tommy. It looks like your daddy could be a little hostile."

"What does that mean?" I whispered back.

"It means he might be having some unfriendly feelings."

"Yeah, you never know when he's not going to be friendly," I said.

"He sure covers it well," she said. "I didn't see that coming." She looked back toward Bobby, whose cola was still half full.

"Della, do you think it's because my dad had to be friendly to nice people and unfriendly to bad people when he was a policeman?" I asked.

"That could be it, Tommy." Della had walked me over to the blue plate special table. "Tommy, I want to give you something so you'll never forget Della's Diner." She pulled out the newest, brightest-blue plate from halfway down one of the stacks. She stood wiping the plate with it pressed against her stuck-out hip.

Still standing back at the table, Bobby stared at my new plate. I think he was jealous that he didn't get one. He was so sad that his eyes looked dazed, still fixed on Della's hip even after she handed me the plate.

"Now, Tommy, when you sit down and say the blessing over the fixings your momma puts on this blue plate, you give Della a thought."

"You mean you want me to pray for you every time I eat?"

"That would be nice of you to remind the good Lord that I could use a little help here. No, Tommy, but I'd be blue if I thought that you would ever forget Della. Now run to the car before your daddy gets upset."

I didn't have to really pee, but I wanted her to know that I knew some grown-up words. "Della, can I use the toilet, I need to urine."

She smiled with a little laugh. "You go right ahead and urine while I walk Bobby to the car."

When I opened the restroom door, I could feel and hear paper rubbing across the old, discolored tile floor. Two of Ronny's writing pads got stuck under the door when I pushed it open. The rest were ripped in half, in the bottom of the wire basket that was lying on its side from Dad's push. I had to dump it over to get 'em out. That basket was taller than my arm was long. I picked up all the pieces and put them on my new plate. I had to hurry; I sure didn't want to hear Dad honk the horn. I didn't know how to get to Florida.

I kept trying and trying to get the pads out from under the door. The harder I pulled, the tighter they got. *Ronny should have made them only five pages thick instead of ten,* I thought. The pads were full of writing, and I needed to get them so he wouldn't be sad. My mom used to say, "If you've tried and tried and don't succeed, you're not praying hard enough." Mom's favorite prayer line that I heard her say the most was, "Oh, dear Lord, please give me the strength . . ." I was sitting on the floor leaning with my shoulder against the door as it slammed shut and the pads popped out. "It worked!" I screamed. Now that was a saying. Mom was right again.

I filled the plate and pressed it tight against my stomach, making sure none of the papers showed as I ran out and down the hall.

Della was back at the order window.

"Hey, Della, when this plate gets old, can I come back and get a new one?" I had slowed down to side shuffling. I looked back at her for an answer.

"You sure can."

"Goodbye, Della."

"So long, Tommy. You be a good boy for your momma now."

"Okay, Della, guess what? You don't have to pray for help. Just pray for strength."

Right as my foot hit the breezeway I heard the short double honk. Through the loose, wavy screen, I could see the back of the car getting farther away. It was still on the sandy, pine-needle-covered, one-way road but headed for the blacktop. Lucky for me Dad had to go slow because of the fan-shaped bushes hitting the sides of the car. If they scratched the car, I was sure I would actually get to feel the "unfriendly feelings of hostile."

Bobby yelled, "Leave that little half-pint here! Go faster, Dad. He's catching up."

When I got even with the door, Mom was yelling for Dad to stop the car, saying that he was scaring me. He had to stop right before turning onto the main road because of a couple of oncoming trucks. *Oncoming* was a new way to use *on* and *coming* for me. Ronny explained that Dad would blink the headlights to let the truck or car in front of us know that we wanted to pass and go around them. The driver in front would blink his lights to let Dad know that it was okay or safe. Every time Dad would go to pass, Mom would say, "Make sure there's no oncoming traffic," when she should have said, "no traffic coming." I wondered why Bobby hadn't corrected her by now.

Mom opened her door and pulled the seat up, and I dove across Bobby. I twisted in the air so as to land on my butt over on my side of the pillow. Bobby tangled my right leg with his left and slugged me in the calf.

"Why did you do that?" I asked, almost crying.

"You know the rules; you were on the wrong side of the Rubicon."

"I had to get in the car!"

"Not from this side, you didn't."

"That was my ranned-over bad leg, and that hurt!"

"I know. It was supposed to hurt."

"The muscle is still smaller than the other, but when it grows back, I bet it won't hurt me then."

"Well, when it grows back, I'll be glad to test it for you."

I didn't think that was funny, but it made Ronny smile.

Blue Plate Special

Verse
They say you haven't lived till ya did the blue plate special
Served every afternoon at Della's Diner
From a converted house on the back road out of Macon
Address 222 Montgomery Lane

Verse
I used to be the only one who ate there
Besides the children and a live-in mother-in-law
But a blinkin' sign says Della's Diner's open
Address truckers' home away from home

Chorus
So step right up and order the blue plate special
I know that the taste of the food and the price is right
But remember Della's taken, so truckers if I were you
I'd make sure that what I order was written on the menu

Verse
I know she walks like a tease, free and easy
With her Coke-bottle figure full of class
But the price you'd have to pay would set you way behind
If I ever caught you with Della putting in overtime

Chapter 7
You Make Me Feel Without a Touch

"Okay, settle down back there, boys," Mom said. "We still have a long way to go."

"Bobby whacked me on my bad leg."

"I'm sure you're going to live," she said.

I hated that saying. Sure I was going to live, but did I have to do it in pain? "I just got my left eyebrow to close up and the dashboard dent in my forehead to start filling in. My kneecap still doesn't feel like it's in place from when he hit me before we even left the driveway. The baseball-size swelling in my calf was gone. Now it's the size of a golf ball and growing again, all because of him."

"That's enough, Tommy. Quit feeling sorry for yourself."

"Sorry? Mom, look at my leg."

"I can't turn around right now. I'll take a look the next time we stop. Bobby, can't you keep him busy for a while without touching or hitting him? And tell him you're sorry."

Bobby put his head back and looked down at me. "Tommy, I'm sorry to say, but saying one is sorry is a sorry thing to have to say."

"Mom, he didn't say he was sorry. He said he was sorry he had to say he was sorry."

"Sorry, Tommy, that'll just have to do for now," Mom said.

Bobby pulled me back in the seat. "Della thinks you're an idiot," he said.

"No, she doesn't. She said I was good in English."

"Look, you numb nut, urine is pee," Bobby said. "The act of relieving yourself of urine is to urinate."

"I don't get it. If urine is pee, and it's okay to say, 'I have to take a pee,' then it's correct to say, 'I have to take a urine.' Right?"

"Peeing is the act of pee, to urinate is the act of urine," Bobby said.

Ronny nudged me with his elbow, arms folded, eyes closed, and said, "Tell the potty expert over there that 'piss on him' is an act that you could say and do."

No way was I going to say that to Bobby. First of all, for some reason he was allowed to cross the Rubicon leading with his wiry arm and fist. Second of all, I was learning new things. I mean, he was at least explaining to me, even though I didn't understand the pee-urine thing. I needed him to tell me the reason for the truck route signs. "Bobby, we never see any signs for car routes. I only see signs for truck routes."

"There aren't any, you spitball," he said. "It's understood. The truck route signs send the trucker around the town, keeping him out of a lot of traffic, then put him back on his route." He pronounced the first one with an *ow* sound, the second with an *ooh* sound.

"So when it's one road with a number, it's a root, but when it's more, it's a route?"

"It's still spelled the same and means the same. It's only pronounced differently, you ignoramus."

Ronny opened his eyes, tilted his head, and looked over toward Bobby. "Do you think Spike's new girlfriend has learned the difference between route and root?"

The wiry arm went flying across the seat and caught Ronny's shoulder with a pop. I didn't understand why Bobby got so mad. It was a simple question; I even wanted to know if she knew.

"Quiet in the back," Dad said. "We're finally here. Look, there's the *Welcome to Florida* sign."

"Yay, we're finally here!" I yelled.

"Sit back, tiny, and shut up," Bobby said. "We still have a long way to go."

"How do you know?" I asked. "You've never been to Florida."

"I know because I can read a map." He pulled one out from under the front seat.

"So what good is that?" I asked.

"Well, look and listen, you little pinhead. I know that Dad has been averaging about fifty miles per hour. Now, on this map's scale, one inch equals a hundred miles." He started pointing and dragging his long, bony finger down the map. He sounded a lot like a teacher. "From where we are right here, down this route to the middle of Florida is a good four inches plus."

"Is Dad taking a root or a route?" I asked.

"That has nothing to do with what we're trying to figure out, you spaghetti head!" Bobby said. "Listen, we average fifty miles per hour, we have four more inches to go on the map, and each inch equals a hundred miles. If this is true we should be there in X hours. What is X?"

"I'm not that stupid. I even know that hours are measured in numbers, not letters."

Bobby's face turned red, and he started biting his lip. He grabbed my leg just above my bad knee and started squeezing, digging his fingers into my bone.

Ronny was smiling big, swallowing back laughter. His ears were moving as he rocked back and forth with every gulping sound.

Bobby put both of his hands around my neck. He pulled my head over and banged his forehead against the side of mine. He pressed his eye to my ear with his mouth on my neck. "It's what I thought," he said.

"What?" I asked.

"It's empty; I can look right through to the other side at your crazy brother, who better knock it off." He turned me loose and let out a deep sigh.

"Why are you mad that Ronny's smiling?" I asked.

"For one thing, he's not sane enough to understand the depth of your inability to problem solve."

I used my T-shirt sleeve to wipe my neck, which solved the problem of Bobby's spit on me. "You're the one with the problem, trying to add numbers and letters together, not me."

"Tommy, you're so slow," he said. "X is the answer that we're looking for."

"No way is X the answer," I said.

Bobby took a big, deep breath and leaned back into his corner. He turned his legs a little toward the Rubicon pillow and crossed them like a girl. He started talking really slow. "X is the symbol used for the unknown answer. In our problem, fifty miles per hour goes into four hundred miles eight times, so X equals eight hours."

"Why X? Why isn't it Y or Z?"

"You can use any dumb letter you want," Bobby said. "That letter will equal the answer. Usually X and Y are used in equations like in finding the square root of a number."

"I get it now. We still have a long way to go because Dad is taking a 'square route' instead of a 'truck route.'"

Bobby pressed the palms of his hands to his forehead, elbows together, and slowly put his head back against the seat. I thought Ronny was going to die from not being able to take a breath.

"Jim, slow down," Mom said. "There's a dead animal in the middle of the road. Look at those big birds eating that carcass!"

"Those big birds just happen to be vultures, and look at that one soar," Bobby said.

"Mom, what kind of animal is a carcass?" I asked.

"The kind we all wish you were," Bobby answered.

"Bobby, you stop talking to him like that!" Mom ordered. "Tommy, a carcass is another name for a dead body."

"Bobby, hey, Bobby," I said.

"Mom said for me not to talk to you anymore, so shut up," he said.

"She didn't say I couldn't talk, so I have one more question. I know you're pretty smart and all that, but tell me how you knew that bird was sore?"

Bobby pulled up on the back of the front seat and put his chin on Mom's shoulder.

"Okay, Mom, he cannot possibly be related to me. Please tell me you picked him up at the orphanage. He is incapable of learning."

"That's it," Mom said. "No more talking. We're almost there."

"And Ronny," Dad added, "you stop rocking and making those horrible laughing noises. You've been going off and on for hours."

"Wait a minute, Mom, what does *incapable* mean?" I asked.

Bobby spoke up. "Mom, let me try to define *incapable* in a manner in which he might understand. Look, retardo."

"No name-calling back there, Bobby," Mom said.

Bobby lowered his voice. "Okay, I know you've never had anyone say you were capable of doing anything."

"No, but I've had teachers ask me if I was *able* to sit still for five minutes," I said.

"Right, and since you are not *able* to do so, you are *incapable* of doing so," he said.

"They just put *in* in front of *capable* and that means I'm not able to do it?"

"That's right. It's called a prefix and when added to the end of the root word, it's called a suffix."

"Now I know you're joking, using the word *root* again," I said.

"Listen to me, you little shit for brains," he whispered. "I'm not joking." He bit his tongue.

"Sorry, your cursing makes me *incapable* of hearing you," I said.

Bobby took a deep breath, grabbed my ear, and started twisting. "Does that help your hearing?"

Ronny was swallowing laughter again. He caught enough sarcastic breath to say, "Don't quit trying. You can teach him. If you give up, you are *capable* of *incapability*."

Bobby sat back and closed his eyes.

"Hey, Ronny, *incapability*, that's a word with a prefix and a suffix, right?" I asked.

"Yeah, it's the root word with a—"

"You're kidding me. Is Bobby right about another root?"

"He's right," Ronny said.

"How do ya remember it all?" I asked. "Is the spelling the same?"

"Don't worry about it. Bobby will spell and even define the definition for you."

"Quiet, before I pound you, punk. I'm trying to catch some Zs," Bobby said.

"Are you dreaming of your Barbie who's using your friend Spike to get over her broken heart?" Ronny asked. "Oh, I'm sorry. Mom always said she was a good girl with an eighteen-karat heart."

"If you really must know, I'm dreaming of Della's long, eighteen-karat legs."

"Bobby, what do you mean by eighteen-carrot legs?" I asked.

His eyelids closed, eyeballs rolling. He grinned slightly, with nostrils flared, as if he could see them, and if he could reach out and maybe touch them. "It stands for the purity of the girls in my life," he replied, maintaining his lost, needy look.

"So it has nothing to do with vegetables?" I asked.

"Nothing at all," he said. "The carrot you're thinking of is spelled differently, and by the way, it is a root."

"Is that true, Ronny?"

"That's true, Tommy."

Mom started pointing out the window. "Look, boys, look! We're crossing the Saint Johns River. Right over there is your father's hometown of Sanford."

After crossing the bridge we turned left and started riding alongside the river. It opened up into a big lake called Lake Monroe right next to the downtown area.

"Jim, does it look any different from when you left here as a teenager?" Mom asked.

"The river looks wider, and the lake looks bigger, but the rest doesn't look much different."

Well, it sure looked different to me. The first thing I couldn't believe was a house built on telephone poles sticking up out of the water. It was called the VFW Post. Dad said it was like a club. I planned on joining the next day just to check it out. We had to pull over one last time to let Mildred out to go. Dad stopped right by a dirt road that led out into the water, to what he said was the band shell.

"What do they do there?" I asked.

"Bands play there in the evening sometimes. For example, if someone is playing the piano, the sound bounces off the half shell out toward the audience."

"So when Clarence comes to visit, he can play with Ronny in the shell?" I asked.

"Clarence is *not* coming here," he said, "and hopefully he's only playing with himself."

There was a zoo right next to City Hall. No charge to get in because you could see the animals from the street anyway. Two blocks up was a big square clock with a face on all four sides. It stood ten foot high right in the middle of the main downtown intersection.

"I can't remember a time when all four of those clocks had the same time on them," Dad said.

"Well, it's about time that someone takes the time to fix the time," Bobby said. He wasn't as good as Ronny at making things rhyme.

While waiting for the light to change, the clock changed. The big hand clicked to the next black dot.

"There goes another minute you'll never get back," Dad said.

"So what?" I said. "It's only a minute."

"Because minutes make hours, and hours make days, and days come to an end for everyone. You get to use a minute for only a minute, so use it wisely."

"I've never thought about time like that," I said. "Have you, Bobby?"

"Yes, but Dad's wrong," Bobby answered. "When sitting in this backseat with you, every minute lasts an hour. If it goes on much longer, I can only hope my days come to an end. All the time I've wasted with you and your weak-minded, crazy brother in the back of this car is gone. I can't buy it back."

"I have to send Homer a postcard because he said, 'If you have money, you can buy anything.'"

"You're really not going to waste time writing to tell Sissy Katz that money can't buy him time, are you?"

"Yes, I am. He's my friend. He also needs to know it's not wise for him to waste another minute trying to learn how to skate."

There were banks on two of the corners and drugstores on the other two. The streets were really different, made with red bricks, bricks that were a lot brighter than the ones they made buildings out of in Cincinnati.

"Look at the street," Dad said. "For a split second, when the sun hit it just right, it looks like it's paved with gold."

Ronny looked out the window. Under his breath he said, "After a bowel movement, my ass looks golder than that street does."

"Oh my," Mom said, "a Sears, Roebuck catalog store right next to a five-and-dime. Look, the ten-cent store is right across the street too."

"That store doesn't sell anything for a nickel, but this one does?" I asked. "I'm sure they both have things for less and for more than a dime," Mom said. "It's called competition."

"It's called capitalism," Ronny said.

"Really, we didn't know that," Bobby said, with his wise mouth. "We thought it was communism or socialism."

"Bobby, why do you have to be so sarcastic to him all the time?" Mom asked.

Ism *must be the suffix for big words,* I thought. "Yeah, Bobby, you are so *sarcastic-ism.*"

"No, Tommy, he's full of *sarcasm,*" Mom corrected.

"You mean he's full of shit," Ronny said.

"Oh, dear Lord, please tell me, where did I go wrong?"

Okay, I was in the middle. Dad was going to come around with a back-handed right. Or Bobby would come across me swinging left and right. Instead, as Dad turned right onto Sanford Avenue, I could see the corner of his mouth turned up. Wow, maybe it was going to be different living there. Ronny cursed, and Dad smiled.

"Look, nothing but Negroes on this street," Ronny said.

"This is downtown Colored Town," Dad said. "This is where they shop and eat, and they get their hair cut right there."

Sure enough, there was Fred's Barber Shop with a sign in the window that said *Colored only.* Right next door was the Army Navy Surplus Store.

"Bobby, you should have kept your Cincinnati army cot," I said. "You can't buy one here—you're too white—unless all your freckles grow together."

"Quit with your dumb-isms, little boy," Bobby said.

"From here east to Mellonville Avenue and south to Celery Avenue is called Georgetown, where the colored stay," Dad said. "Your grandparents live on Mellonville, but on the other side of Celery."

"Why such funny names for streets, and can the colored people cross Celery Avenue if they want?" I asked.

"Sanford is nicknamed Celery City," Dad replied. "It's the celery capital of the world. If a Negro is working the crops across in the Chases' fields, it's okay to cross Celery Avenue. A Negro can go where the whites live, but he better have a good reason for being there when the police stop and ask him."

"What if a colored boy has to go that way to get to school or something?"

"They have their own downtown, schools, neighborhoods, playgrounds—even their own sitting area in the balcony at the movies."

"Sometimes during the cowboy and Indian fights, I like to be in the front row," I said. "They never get to sit down in the front?"

"No, and that's considered 'separate but equal,'" Bobby said. "I guess you could say this is your 'segregation-ism' at its best."

Right then I knew that the *ism* words were really going to help my vocabulary.

We reached the cross streets of Celery and Mellonville. The sign read, *The Corner Store.*

"Great name for that store being right on the corner," I said.

"That's so creative," Bobby said, like a smart aleck.

"I think it's great *creative-ism,*" I piped up.

Ronny jabbed his right elbow into my ribs. "Knock off the *ism* crap."

"That's your new delicatessen," Dad said.

It wasn't new, and it looked nothing like Johnny's. It had two old Texaco gas pumps in front. They'd been there since Dad was a kid back in the twenties. The store looked kind of like Della's—a wooden house but without the breezeway porch, and it had two stories. The couple who owned the store lived in the top one.

"Look," I said, pointing, "the fruits and vegetables are outside in baskets."

"Those aren't baskets," Mom said. She broke out singing, "A bushel and a peck and a hug around the neck." It was the happiest she'd been since we left Cincinnati.

There were two restroom doors along the side of the store. One said *White only* and the other said *Colored*. But there was only one water fountain, marked *White only.*

"Look, Bobby, separate-but-equal toilets but no colored water fountain."

"They use the hose right there next to the fountain," Dad said.

"That's not the same, is it, Bobby?"

"Tommy, nobody has died from drinking out of a hose," Dad said.

"That's why they call it segregation," Bobby said.

"That's right, Bobby. That's true se-gre-gation—"

"Put *ism* on the end of that, and you'll lose a tooth," Ronny said.

I had to finish it. I couldn't stop myself. I put my hands over my face, my head down between my legs, and added *ism.*

Ronny brought his forearm down hard across my back. I was crying and yelling when we pulled into our grandparents' driveway, which was nothing but sand.

"Tommy, stop it!" Mom said. "We're finally here. It's the end of the longest, worst, and most miserable trip I have ever been on."

My back was killing me, but what Mom said hurt me with surprise. I wondered how she could say something like that. The trip was the best thing that had ever happened to me.

Not on purpose, but because I couldn't read very well, or hardly at all, I learned by observing and questioning. I watched the actions and reactions of others and listened. The experience from that closed-in, backseat trip gave me great insight into my little world. I learned that my mother had a great understanding of love. She didn't need Webster's Dictionary. She had her own definition, which I believed might have been learned from a broken heart or two. I didn't understand the real emotional breaking of a heart but could tell that Mom was an expert. I didn't know if Dad could pick up the pieces, or if he even knew it needed fixing.

I learned that Dad was hard to figure. He was looking for answers about the before and afterlife. At least that's what I picked up from his growing interest in religion. I didn't care. I was just glad to be living. Ronny and I talked about the Bible, religion, and Dad's preacher hunting. Ronny said he hoped Dad would ease up on the "kick your son's ass or spoil the child" scripture. I knew *ass* was in the Bible but not in that verse. He got it mixed up with the "working on the Sabbath with your ass in mud" scripture. I learned that Bobby thought Ronny was crazy.

Dad turned the car off, put it in park, and began lecturing Ronny on how he needed to act. "Now hear this, Ronny, before you—"

"Why can't you just say it to all three?" Mom interrupted, but not looking at Dad. Her fists were clenched at the sides of her hips, and she looked down at the floorboard. "The other two back there aren't angels, you know!"

"Bobby thinks he is," I said.

"Damn it! You're not getting out of this car until all of you promise me—"

Bobby gave me a short, sharp elbow poke to the side of the chest.

"Don't touch him, Bobby."

"He's still touching my leg," I said.

"Tommy, that's enough," Mom said. "Mind your own beeswax. You're always up in someone else's business. Start minding your own. That's it; until I hear you apologize to one another, you will sit in this car. Come on, Jim. You three stay in that backseat and decide who's going to say 'I'm sorry' first." Mom closed her door and walked toward the house.

Mom was right to say something to Dad. Not only had I been watching, listening, and questioning, I was also feeling—that is, feeling Ronny slipping away. He was talking less, with more cursing and anger in his voice when he did speak. I hoped it was from being homesick for Cincy and missing his friend Clarence. I knew he'd get over it because of Mom's saying that "time cures all." The hickey from Dad's ring was still on the back of my head, so I knew it could take a while for Ronny to feel better.

"Dad, when Mom cusses, that means she's really mad," I said.

"If I've told you boys once, I've told you a hundred times: you could be absolutely stupid and get along just fine in this world if you would just do what I say."

"Dad, Ronny didn't do anything. It was Bobby who hit me after I said he thought he was an angel."

"I'm sure he's done something," Dad said, as he pulled Mildred out from between Ronny's legs. "Mom or I will check on you. Do not get out of the car. Ronny, that includes you."

"Dad, Bobby is still touching me."

Dad just walked away.

"No, I'm not."

"Can you make me feel without a touch? The answer's no, right?"

"You're being touched because you have crossed the Rubicon. Now the die is cast. This is the point where deliberation ends and action begins."

"What does that mean?" I asked.

"It means he's deliberately touching you for the action," Ronny said.

"Keep quiet, you sicko," Bobby said.

Ronny said every word as he wrote it down. "You make me feel without a touch. You're turning me on. You're giving me thoughts I thought were gone." Then he put his pen and paper back in his pocket.

Bobby sat biting his lip and bouncing his left knee up and down.

Ronny sat on the edge of the seat looking straight ahead. He glanced over at Bobby every few seconds.

"Don't do it," Bobby said.

"Ronny, what do you think about the 'absolutely stupid' thing?" I asked. Ronny didn't answer.

"Tommy, Dad is telling you to be obedient: to obey him, to obey authority, to obey the rules," Bobby said.

"What's the difference between just being stupid and absolutely . . ."

Ronny leaned up over the front seat and opened the door. "I'm going to see about Mildred," he said and jumped out.

"There you go. There's your example of absolutely stupid and just plain stupid," Bobby said.

Ronny went around the back of the house.

"Bobby, do you think he's going to get in trouble?" I asked.

"Of course he is."

"I'd like to be smart, but I think I'm going to give up on the school learning, reading, and spelling stuff," I said.

"Why?" Bobby asked.

"Because it's really hard, and if Mom tells me that Dad is telling the truth, I'm going to do it."

"You're going to do what?"

"You and lots of others say I'm stupid. If I can get to 'absolutely stupid' and just do what Dad says, I'll get along just fine in this world, right?"

"Wrong," Bobby said. "Dad isn't going to be here forever to tell you what to do."

"Are you kidding me?" I said. "If he and Mom go back to Cincinnati, I'm going too."

"Go ahead with your plan. You've reached 'absolutely.'"

"I'm sorry, Bobby. Now, tell me you're sorry so we can go in and tell Mom."

Dad came out from behind the house holding Ronny by the back of the neck. He pushed him toward the car. Ronny couldn't keep his balance in the sand and fell forward with both arms stretched out, landing hard on the hood.

"You better hope you didn't put a dent in that car," Dad yelled. "Get in and stay there till I tell you to get out." He pointed at us. "You two get in the house."

"Dad, I told Bobby I was sorry, but he didn't tell me he was," I said.

"Maybe it's because he's smart but thinks he's wise and is starting to hearken unto no one but himself," Dad said.

"What does *hearken* mean?" I asked.

"It means to listen and obey," Dad answered. "It means if you don't start bad habits, you don't have to break 'em." He held the front door to the house open. "Now get in, sit on that couch over there, and keep quiet."

Bobby and I sat down on the couch.

Dad went straight to the back room, where I could hear Mom talking softly to someone.

"*Hearken* has a long definition, doesn't it, Bobby?"

"*Hearken* is the biblical word for *listen*. The rest must be one of Dad's new sayings that he just threw in there."

I knew I'd heard that word before. "What's the name of that Christmas song?" I asked.

"You mean 'Hark! The Herald Angels Sing'?"

"That's it. *Hark* means to 'listen' to the angels sing."

"Tommy, that's right. Very good! Right when I think you're absolutely—"

"So when we become angels, you'll sing with the Bobbys, Ronny will sing with the Ronnys, I'll sing with the—"

"It's herald angels, not Harold," Bobby said.

"They sound exactly the same," I said. "What's the difference?"

"Oh, nothing. A couple of letters and, of course, the meaning of the word."

"Bobby, I'm pretty sure that just doing what Dad says might be a whole lot easier for me."

"I'm beginning to think you're right."

It had been at least ten minutes, and Mom and Dad were still in the back room talking.

"Hey, Dad, can Ronny get out of the car now?" I yelled.

"You better sit down and keep quiet," Bobby said. "Something's wrong."

I went over, opened the front door, and started dancing and making faces at Ronny. Dad came up behind me and flicked my ear. At the same time Ronny stuck his arm out the window and gave me the finger. My back stopped hurting from Ronny's forearm slam, now that my ear was stinging.

"Like your Mother said, you need to mind your own business. You're starting bad habits like your brother, and I'm going to go break one of his right now."

Staying a few feet behind, I followed Dad out to the car. He reached in and pulled Ronny's arm out the window. He twisted his hand, bending his middle finger back.

Ronny, with a short, gasping squeal and the sound of a bubblegum pop from his finger, fell back in the seat.

"That's a bad habit you don't want to start," Dad said as he walked back to the house.

The saying was, "If you don't start bad habits, you don't have to break them." It said nothing about breaking bones.

Ronny was doing something strange for Ronny: he was crying. But I knew exactly what he needed. I ran into the kitchen. "Bobby, come in here and wet a cold dish towel for Ronny!"

"What did he do now?" Bobby asked.

"He's starting bad habits, so Dad's breaking his fingers."

I grabbed the soaking-wet towel from Bobby's hands and ran to the car. "Here, Ronny, wrap this around your hand. I'm going to go tell Mom on Dad."

"No, Tommy, not a word."

"Look at your finger. It's crooked and getting fat."

He pressed the wet dish towel to his eyes, wiped his face, and pulled his finger straight out till it snapped.

"Here, take this towel back and tell Bobby not to tell Mom."

"But . . ."

"But nothing, Tommy. Just obey me for once and do what I tell you. Mom doesn't need to know."

"She needs to know 'not to start any bad habits.' I'll tell ya that."

Bobby was now sitting at the end of the hard, plastic-covered couch closest to the back room. He had his long neck stretched out trying to hear what was being said.

I tossed the towel into the kitchen sink, came back into the front room, and sat down next to him without saying a word.

He quietly said, "Sit down and shut up before I give you a knuckle sandwich."

I started to explain to him that I was already sitting down and hadn't said anything. Before I could put the *ism* on the end of "You're losing your smart-ism," he had his right arm wrapped around the back of my head. He delivered a left-handed sandwich punch to my forehead. I tried to yell, but I couldn't get my breath. He was holding my mouth shut and pinching my nose closed with his thumb and long pointer finger. I ran out of air, and things were turning black. I was hot and felt like I was about to fall asleep when I heard Dad's voice. It sounded like he was far away.

Bobby had pushed me down on the couch. My hot, sweaty cheek was sticking to the plastic cushion. From my lying-down position I could only see Dad from his waist down. His pants, along with the floor, looked a little blurry. He reached down, barely pressing the back of his hand to the side of my face. His voice was clearer, now that I had air back in my ears. But the sound was different: softer, lighter, and kind of unsure.

"My daddy died last night. We have to take your grandmother to the funeral parlor to make arrangements. You boys be good now."

Mom came out with her arm around Grandma, who was wearing a black shawl over her rounded back and shoulders. She had it pulled over her head, her face toward the floor.

"I tell ya, Irene, he was a God-fearing man," Grandma said.

"Tommy, you mind Bobby, and no fighting," Mom said. "We'll be back shortly."

"Don't let that dog eat my yard birds," Grandma added.

I peeled my cheek from the sticky plastic and sat up just like Bobby, with my head back and hands down flat on the couch next to my legs. I stayed quiet for a couple of minutes. Then I told him, "You almost killed me."

"What makes you think that?" he said. "You're still talking, aren't you?"

"Yeah, and I really wanted to talk to Grandpa. Did you ever get to talk to him?"

"On the phone a couple of times to thank him for the crate of oranges he always sent us at Christmastime."

"What did it feel like?" I asked.

"What did what feel like?"

"To talk to a God-fearing man," I asked.

"Right now, I'm tired, and I'm the only one you need to fear," he said.

"You're not God."

"You're going to need God more than you know if you don't shut up."

Yeah, he was tired, but I could tell from his cracking voice, he was also sad. We sat side by side, heads back, looking up at the water-stained ceiling. "Bobby, can I ask you one more question? Then I'm going to go out back and check this place out."

"It better not be something dumb," he said.

"No, look, I don't understand."

"That's an understatement."

"*Understatement.* I've never heard you use that word before."

"It's the opposite of overstatement, and you better make your statement quick or get out," he said.

"Okay, I've wondered this before. If the Bible tells us that God is good and God is great, why does it tell us to fear him?"

"I know it sounds like contradicting statements, if you will, but to fear God means to obey him," he explained.

"Does everything lead back to obeying?"

"Yes, so obey me and leave me alone for a while."

"What do you want me to do?"

"Tommy!" he yelled.

"You said 'If you will' after you said 'contradicting statements,' but you never finished. So will I do what?"

He got up and walked out the door.

In my mind I could hear one of Mom's sayings. *Tommy, it's okay to be alone. Everyone needs alone time.* I remember staying on the couch, in my leaned-back position, and closing my eyes. I started thinking of one thing after another that I had learned. Things like Dad was once a kid too. That he had a daddy instead of a dad. That maybe Bobby needed some peace and quiet, just like Mom did when she watched television. I tried to picture the trip like a movie. This way it would help me to remember not only what was said, but who said it, and why, when, and where.

You Make Me Feel Without a Touch

Verse
Honey, you have inspired more dreams than you know
From your sexy smile and your eyes that glow
The special thing about you is that you haven't a clue
What you make me do from the way that you move

Chorus
You make me feel without a touch
You're turning me on
You're giving me thoughts I thought were gone
Is it that you don't try at all
That makes me want you so much?
You make me feel without a touch

Verse
I wonder what would happen if I came on to you
And you opened up your heart saying you love me too
Could we keep that first-time feeling like when love is all
    brand new?
Would I still get excited just from the sight of you?

Chorus Repeat

Tag
Oh honey, you make me feel without a touch

Chapter 8
Stepping Out, Movin' On
Urp, Slop, Bring the Mop

Maybe the tent preacher was right when he prayed, in his loudest voice, "Dear Lord, please help us to never forget what we have learned here this night, so that we may take it and use it in our daily lives. Amen and amen!"

That's what I was going to do. If every day I copied what I learned from watching and listening, why worry about reading? Besides, this way I wouldn't have to be absolutely stupid and do only what Dad said.

Mildred started barking. I got up, went through the kitchen, out the back door, and onto the porch. Bobby was sitting in a rocking chair watching Ronny throw oranges left-handed against the side of an old wooden shed.

Ronny had his right hand, with the broken finger, stuck in his back pocket. "Bobby, I need you to find me a Popsicle stick and some tape," he said.

"Find it yourself," Bobby said. "I'm not your maid. Who died and left you boss?"

The "breaking bad habits" saying didn't stop Ronny. He managed to pull his hand out and give Bobby a swollen, broken finger.

Bobby got up with the rocking chair still rocking and jumped off the two-foot-high wooden porch. "Is that your age or your IQ?" he asked, as he walked away toward the front of the house.

It was a rockin' back yard. There were three rows, twelve trees deep, of orange, tangerine, and grapefruit trees. There was also a row of fruit trees called guavas. I thought that was a funny name for a fruit. Ronny told me to eat one to see what it tasted like. One bite and I gagged and spit it out. It was soft, mushy, and a lot worse than fruitcake.

Mildred had stopped barking.

"Ronny, where's Mildred?" I asked.

"Down at the chicken pen," he answered.

I ran to the end of the row, slipping and sliding on rotten guavas. There lay Mildred, her head resting on her front paws and her tail wagging, watching the chickens. Their heads bobbed as they walked freely in and out of the holes in the pen.

At that time, the count was thirty chickens and one mean, loud rooster. I would end up with Grandpa's old job of gathering the eggs. It was more like hunting the eggs. There were nests everywhere. Some were under palm trees, some by the fruit trees. Most were in, under, and even on top of the coop. I would clean the eggs and put them in a straw basket marked *fresh eggs*. Just as Grandpa had done for years, we swapped them at the Corner Store.

The owner would only trade us milk, bread, and butter for the eggs. I guessed that was still a good deal because Dad would say, "Good job, Tommy. That's one less dollar I'll have to spend."

It really wasn't a job. I mean, I didn't get paid. It was just something that had to be done day after day, month after month, so I did it. But I had no idea what a valuable lesson I would eventually learn because of those chickens.

Mildred and I walked back through the grove to the house. Ronny sat on the edge of the porch with his legs dangling. He was taping his two middle fingers together with a cherry-stained Popsicle stick. It was sunny, hot, and sticky. Mildred went between his legs and under the porch, dug out a hole, and lay down.

"Where did you get that Popsicle stick," I asked.

"Are you writing a book?"

"Of course not. If I can't read one, I'm sure not writing one. Come on in. I want to show you something."

"I'm not allowed. I have to stay out here till they get back. What did you want to show me?"

"You gotta see the plastic couch. I was able to wipe the sweat from my cheek right off it with my T-shirt."

"So what?"

"So it won't matter if you have one of your heavy-sleeper

nights on that couch. Whiz-bang, you wipe it off with your shirt or dish towel and throw it in the washer. No one will know. Unless you think Grandma already knows, and she had the couch covered just for you."

Ronny got up slowly, walked over, bent down, and picked up an orange with his left hand. Before the screen door could swing closed behind me, I felt a hard, wet explosion on the back of my shoulder. The orange flew apart all over the kitchen. "Now there's a whiz-bang for you," Ronny said.

"I don't know why you're mad. I was just letting you know about the couch." Then in my sissy voice, I said, "You're still a baby. If you would wake up at night, you could 'push the button, pull the chain, and watch your pee-pee go down the drain.'"

After I had said my smart little rhyme, I didn't feel so good. Ronny sat down in the grass with his back against the old shed, looking sad.

I came back out to the edge of the porch. "I have to admit that was a good shot," I said.

"Just go back inside. Don't try to kiss up to me."

"No, really, you threw that left-handed. I'm left-handed, and I can't throw that good. Look at the orange spots on the wood above your head. All of your practice throws are close together. You should have stayed in Cincinnati and pitched for the Reds."

"Tommy, get lost for a while."

"If you don't get Grandma's kitchen cleaned up before they get back, you're the one that better get lost."

Since Ronny couldn't come in the house, I picked up the big pieces off the floor. Wiping the stove off with the wet dish towel did nothing but smear the orange into juice. Bobby was sitting on the couch finishing up the other half of the Popsicle.

"Hey, can you come help me clean this up?" I asked.

"Me?" Bobby said, as he sucked the last cherry-red bite from the stick. "Let me once again inform you of the reoccurring circumstances. This situation is perhaps new and different, but in retrospect, it's one and the same with you and Crazy outside there. It's the game of disobedience and its consequences."

"Does that mean you're going to help or not?"

"It means that I had nothing to do with the movement that caused the ballistic projectile of the orange," he said.

"Can't you just say yes or no?"

"I already did."

"No, you didn't."

"Yes, I did."

"No, you didn't."

"Yes, I did."

"No . . ."

"Yes . . ."

"No . . ."

"Open, I'm thirsty," were the words of my little sister at the front door.

They were back. The door opened, and Dad walked in, went straight back to the kitchen, opened the icebox, and pulled out the pitcher of water. "What happened here?" he asked, as he pulled some of the sticky pulp from the bottom of his shoe.

"Well, I shouldn't have," I said, "but I opened the door, and an orange bounced off my shoulder and into the kitchen. I'm cleaning it up right now."

Dad looked at Bobby, who was still on the couch chewing on the Popsicle stick.

"It only happened a few minutes ago," Bobby said. "From what I could tell, he was teasing Ronny about wetting the bed. Ronny got mad and hit him with the orange."

"It was my fault," I said.

"He's older," Dad said. "He should know better, and he does wet the bed."

"But I made him throw it, tond he hasn't wet the bed since we left Cincinnati."

Dad looked at me, shook his head, took his belt off, and walked out the back door.

"For your information, we haven't been in a bed since we left Cincinnati," Bobby said.

"So he hasn't peed the bed then, right? See, Bobby, you

don't know everything."

Dad had laid his belt across the back of the rocking chair. Maybe he didn't use it because it wasn't big like his police belt. Instead, he walked over and picked three firm oranges from off a tree. Ronny hadn't moved. He was still sitting on the grass, back against the shed, with bent knees pulled to his chest.

"You always have to learn the hard way, don't you? Everyone else has to behave but you, right? The rules don't pertain to you, do they? They're made for all the other people, aren't they? You don't have to stop at a stop sign when you're turning right, do you? You can just slow down a little and keep on rolling, can't you? Stop only means 'stop' for the other guy, doesn't it? Everybody should be obedient but Ronny."

Dad asked all those questions so fast that Ronny didn't even have time to answer yes or no. Boy oh boy, was I confused. First of all, what did driving have to do with throwing an orange? I knew Ronny had to be really mixed up. He had never turned right at a stop sign. He wasn't even old enough to drive.

"We've only been here a few hours, and already you've learned that you like to throw oranges," Dad told him. "So much so, that even a broken finger didn't stop you."

I was on the porch standing behind the rocking chair. I was trying to see how hard I could rock it without it falling over. At the same time the rocker tumbled off the porch, a hole went through the old weathered shed. It hit a few inches above Ronny's head. He didn't budge an inch.

"Stand up, turn around, and put your hands against the shed," Dad said. "You know the routine."

Ronny stood up, and as he turned around, I could see sadness in his eyes and on his face, but no fear.

"Let's see how it feels to be hit in the back with an orange," Dad said. He wound up like the Reds' Joe Nuxhall from the mound.

"Don't, Dad!" I yelled.

He let it fly, hitting Ronny right between the shoulder blades.

Ronny arched his back and fell to his knees.

"Get up and assume your familiar position," Dad said.

Ronny used his hands to crawl back up to the side of the shed.

"Dad, that was a hard orange," I said. "The one he threw at me was soft and almost rotten. It didn't hurt like that, and he threw it left-handed too."

"Some people learn obedience the easy way. Your brother chooses to learn how to obey the hard way." He winged the third orange sidearm from about fifteen feet away.

The orange crushed into the middle of Ronny's low back, and he slid to the ground.

"Now you've been hit twice. So if I were you, I would think twice before I picked up another orange." Dad wiped his hands on his pants and walked back into the house.

Ronny stood up, but he stayed bent forward like a pitcher looking for the signal from the catcher. He said his leg burned like an electric shock from the last fastball. I still got that sick feeling in my stomach for Ronny, even though he said he might, could, and would kill me if he had to.

I guess it was because I loved him, at least according to Mom's definition. I mean, I did care when he felt bad, was hurt, or sick. It made me mad when adults talked about him behind his back. I respected him for being able to withstand the cruel things they would say and not say. They would say he talked funny, he had a horrible laugh, his ears were big, and that they couldn't see his nose for the freckles. He never heard anyone say he was a handsome young man or even a cute kid. Regardless, he was able to look strong and appeared sure of himself.

Another favorite saying of Mom's was this: "Find out if she takes care of her feet. If she does, then you can be pretty sure she takes care of everything else." She also said, "Find out what side of the tracks she lives on and what her father does for a living." That was Mom's way of gaining some basic knowledge of someone.

As far as having knowledge of someone, nobody knew Ronny like I did. I knew that he washed his feet as much as I did because we used the same bathwater. I knew what his dad did for a living and what side of the tracks he lived on. I knew that Ronny had a big heart, which had been broken many times at a very young age. I also knew he had the ability to have feelings for others. In a weird way, he didn't want to let it be known, but he had feelings for me too. He watched out for me. He would say it was only because Mom said it was his job, but I knew he had to have loved me too. After all, he had spared my life more than once.

According to Mom, the more knowledge you had about a person's past, the better you could understand why they acted the way they did. It gave you insight into why they might see the world from a different viewpoint. Knowledge or not, I didn't understand the "understanding" part of Mom's definition of love when it came to Ronny. I didn't understand why he didn't get mad or didn't show it. Why he didn't tell Mom how he felt or go to her for comfort like I did. Why he didn't speak up for himself or openly fight back. Why or how he kept from crying even when I knew he was hurting. I knew Ronny wasn't an angel, but I wondered if with some understanding from Dad, he just might have been.

~~~

Over the next couple of hot summer months, Ronny's finger healed up and his back got better. Somehow he managed to hide his wounds from Mom.

We had been to a different church every week because Dad took Sundays off from work. I didn't know why it mattered which church we attended. It seemed like every sermon was about obedience.

The last one was the First Baptist Church preaching, "Obey the Ten Commandments or burn in hell. Obey the law of tithing or you will burn in the last days. Obey your mother and father, or your days will not be long upon this land."

While sitting there, I asked Ronny, "Why is this called the first?"

"Because there are fifty, and we have forty-nine churches to go."

I watched and listened. If I learned something, I planned
~~~

to "use it in my daily life," like in the old tent-preacher's prayer. But even I didn't need to hear the same thing forty-nine more times. I whispered, "Ronny, why do we sit *in* pews, but we sit *on* benches? They both feel the same."

"Why is your ass as sore as mine?" he asked.

"You're in trouble," I said. "I bet the Heavenly Father can hear your voice really clear when you cuss in church. I do think more people would come if they had these meetings in the Ritz theaters."

"You're right, Tommy, that's a great idea," he said.

"I'm still telling Mom you said *A-S-S* in church."

"Now you said it."

"No, I didn't. I spelled it."

"You think God can't spell?"

During this time, without even knowing it, I was also learning to love Grandma according to Mom's recipe. The first words she ever said directly to me came right after they finished lowering Grandpa into the ground. I was crying even though I never got to meet or talk to him. We started walking slowly back toward the car. Ronny had stopped to use a headstone to write something down on his pad, and I moved in next to Grandma.

She put her lonely, shaking arm around my shoulders. Her voice was weak, with a soft, Southern kind of rhythmic twang. "Tommy, I hear that you don't like the taste of guavas," she said.

"No, do you?" I asked.

"I've developed a taste for them over the years, but your grandpa really loved them," she said.

We weren't even out of the graveyard yet, and already I wanted to ask Grandpa why.

The next day as I passed through the kitchen on the way out back, Grandma asked, "Tommy, would you like a peanut butter and jelly sandwich?"

I was eleven years old and hadn't had more than a couple of peanut butter sandwiches in my whole life. "I guess I'll try one," I said.

She sat down at the table with me as I ate my newfound, okay sandwich.

"What would you like to talk about?" she asked.

"Did Grandpa really love those guavas?"

"Tommy, fruits are like people. If you give them a chance, you just may learn to love them."

"I could never learn to love those guavas," I said.

"You never know. A little taste here and a little taste there."

That had to be a Southern saying. Grandma had never been out of Florida.

"I heard you learned to love the Navel oranges that Grandpa and I sent you every Christmas. The Temple oranges are out of season right now, but I bet you could learn to love those Valencia oranges out back too."

"Oh yeah, those oranges you sent us were good," I agreed.

I wondered why oranges couldn't just be called oranges. There were enough different names of things to learn already. There was one cool thing I had learned: all the people who died weren't buried in Cincinnati.

Most every afternoon, when Mom took what she called her "going-through-the-change-of-life" nap, Grandma would fix me a peanut butter and jelly sandwich. She would sit at the table, talk, ask me questions, and watch me eat. Every day when I finished eating and she finished talking, she would ask me, "Are you ready to eat a guava today?"

"No way," I would say.

She would smile and laugh a little as she cleared the table. "Maybe tomorrow," she would say.

"Maybe, Grandma, but only maybe," I would answer.

Summer vacation came to an end, and on our first morning of school, Ronny and I caught the school bus down at the Corner Store. We were only the second stop, so there were plenty of empty seats. Ronny sat next to me anyway.

I was glad because I had a few questions. "Ronny, do you think the teachers down here make you read out loud like they do in Cincinnati," I asked.

"Just do the best you can," he said.

"But my best is still the worst."

"If you get laughed at enough, maybe you'll practice

reading more."

"When it comes to the class spelling bees, I'm always picked last, and I'm always the first to have to sit down," I said.

"Did you ever think that just maybe it was because you can't spell?"

"Yeah, but I need to know what came first, so I know what to learn first."

"What do you mean, 'what came first'?" he asked.

"Well, after watching the chickens, it didn't take me long to figure out which came first," I said.

"Really? Do tell."

"Ronny, it's simple," I said. "No chicken equals no egg."

"Do you know how many centuries people have been wanting to know the answer to that question?" he asked.

"Well, that goes to show ya, I've been learning a lot since we left Cincy. So tell me what came first. Do I learn to spell first or read first?"

"If you see a word enough times from reading it, you'll learn how to spell it. If you learn how to spell a word, you'll know it when you see it."

"That's not what I asked you. Mom said, 'Things come in order. The Lord's house is a house of order.'"

"Well, look around," he said. "You're in a small farming town in the middle of Florida. We're far from any Lord's house of order."

I remember feeling frustrated and anxious almost to the point of crying and screaming.

"You'll figure it out. Look how much you've learned since we've gotten to Florida."

"True, but what if it takes me as long to learn to read as it's taking you on the chicken-and-egg thing?"

For some reason Ronny was smiling big at what I had said, when the lady bus driver yelled out, "My name is Mrs. Knott, *K-N-O-T-T.* Do not, *N-O-T,* try any funny business on my bus, or you might find a knot, *K-N-O-T,* on your head. That's the most important spelling lesson you'll get this year."

"Ronny, is *not* spelled that many ways?" I asked.

"Yes."

"Why?"

"Because it is."

"Not, *N-O-T*, could be used all three ways: Mrs. Not, not on your head, and not doing something."

"But it's not *N-O-T*," he said.

"Why not *N-O-T*?" I asked.

"Tommy, do not, *N-O-T*, try to reinvent the wheel. Just oil and polish it when needed."

"That doesn't make any sense," I said. "You can't use one of Dad's sayings."

"Why not, *K-N-O-T*?" he asked.

"That's not the right spelling for that *not*," I said.

"Very good. You're right, it's *N-O-T*, not."

Wow, I thought, this could end up being a tough year with the bus driver teaching spelling too.

"The first drop-off coming up will be Sanford Junior High School. Everyone stays in their seats until the bus comes to a complete stop, and I open the door."

"Tommy, don't miss the home buses, and no fighting the first day of school," Ronny said as he stood up.

He didn't need to worry about me fighting. I wasn't going to mess up my brand new Chuck Taylor All Stars.

Mom and Grandma had taken me and Ronny shopping, making me try on new pants and shirts. Mom would say I looked "snazzy," and Grandma said I looked like a "snappy tune." I had to make a choice between a new shirt and pants or the shoes. Mom said one or the other because she didn't want me to get spoiled. I knew it was because of the cost. I had pants and shirts that I thought were good enough, so I picked the All Stars.

"Are you sure?" Mom asked. She sang a line from some old church hymn. "Choose the right when a choice is placed before you."

This wasn't a religious choice.

"Ronny, what would you choose?" I asked. "Do I look cool in these All Stars?"

"Oh yeah, you look like a real cool cat." Then he started singing in his new wannabe Southern country voice, "You'll be steppin' out, movin' on, tryin' on boots, tennis shoes, and thongs." At least he wasn't singing that I'd be stepping out looking snazzy and snappy.

The shoes were a better choice than the one Ronny made of standing up before the bus stopped.

"Young man, that bottom of yours better find a seat before it gets kicked off this bus!" Mrs. Knott screamed. "Are you hard of hearing?"

Ronny only made it two rows up and across the aisle before claiming the open seat next to the prettiest girl on the bus. It wasn't by accident that he ended up in that seat. The whole time he had been talking to me, he was staring at her long, blond ponytail. From my angle I could see the side of her perfect Florida-suntanned face. Not even one freckle. I thought it was quite brave of him for a couple reasons. He sat down by her and told her he was new in town. He found out her name and grade and asked for her mother's phone number. *The mother's phone number question was really dumb,* I thought.

The bus stopped, the door opened, and the driver twisted around in her seat. "All junior high students off the bus. All grammar school students stay in your seats."

Ronny got up, smiled back at me, and headed up the aisle with a pair of pretty, tan legs walking right behind him.

"You stand right over here, young man." Mrs. Knott grabbed Ronny by the arm and pulled him over next to her seat. "Honey, you go right ahead," she said to the girl.

The ponytail bounced down the steps and off the bus.

"What's your name?" asked Mrs. Knott.

"It's Johnny Ray," Ronny said. "Johnny Ray Hickenboch."

"Well, Johnny Ray," she said, "let's not get started off on the wrong foot on the first day of school. Tomorrow you get up on the right side of the bed and put your right foot forward. And don't act like you can't hear me back there, not with those big ears. Now get off the bus. You're holding up traffic."

That could be my problem. Not only did I kick left-footed, I was left-handed. My bed was against the wall, so I got up on the left side every morning. I was pretty sure that when I walked, I started out on my left foot. I thought that she could be right. After all, she could spell the same sound three different ways that meant three different things. I knew she had to be the first woman smart enough to ever drive a bus. I had never seen another. Right then I made up my own "first" saying. "I'm going to start out right, so I'll be all right." I spread it around school that year, but it never caught on.

The blond ponytail walked slowly alongside the bus, stopping right below my window. Ronny stepped off the bus acting like he was going the other way.

In a snooty but sweet Southern voice, punctuated with a slight separation of each word, she said, "Hey, why did you want my mother's phone number? It's the same as mine and my daddy's. We live in the same house."

"I want to get permission to call you," he said.

"What are you talking about?" she asked. "I'm allowed to talk to whomever for ten minutes at seven o'clock every night."

"That's exactly the same time and amount that I'm allowed to talk," he said. "I'll get your number later." He started walking away.

"Urp, slop! I don't want to waste my phone time talking to you."

"It doesn't sound like it," he said, looking back over his shoulder.

She paused for a few seconds. "Boy, you're lookin' and talkin' silly." The ponytail was swinging left to right as she shook her head and walked away. Or was it right to left?

I didn't know how Ronny came up with those first two names so fast. Hickenboch was the name of the pond at the south end of Mellonville Avenue. Ronny and I caught our first brim fish there with Grandpa's old cane pole. We brought it home to eat for supper. Grandma said it was too small to cook, but Grandpa would have been very proud of us. I knew he wouldn't have been proud of Ronny's first day on the school bus.

The tires made a rippling sound over the brick streets to

Sanford Grammar School. I started adding up Ronny's sins of fire. He got out of his seat too early, he gave himself a new name, and he lied about having a certain telephone time. Bobby had informed me that there were not fifty Baptist churches, only the First Baptist. That was another lie, and Ronny had told me that one while in the house of the Lord. I was thinking that he might need to hear those "obeying" sermons another forty-nine times.

Finally, we got to school. Riding the bus to junior high first was out of the way. I could walk to school faster, and after the first day, sometimes I did.

As we got off the bus, Mrs. Knott didn't ask one other kid their name, only me. "What's your name, young man?"

"Tommy. Tommy Brooks."

"What's your brother's name? That was your brother sitting by you, wasn't it?"

"Yes, it's Ronny Brooks."

"Interesting," she said. "Ronny Brooks by way of Hickenboch Pond."

Uh-oh, she must have fished there too.

Steppin' Out, Movin' On

Intro (acapella)
Steppin' out, movin' on, trying on boots, tennis shoes, and
    thongs
Dancin' off these lovesick blues in a brand new honky-tonk

Verse
I'm lookin' through the closet for something nice to wear
Tryin' to figure out just how to do my hair
I'll be putting on my makeup while I'm headed out the door
And I hope I look as good as I feel when I hit the old dance
    floor

Chorus
Because I'm steppin' out, movin' on
Tryin' on boots, tennis shoes, and thongs
Dancin' off these lovesick blues
In a brand new honky-tonk

Verse
Go ahead and watch your TV or work on that old car
Make your plans to meet the boys down at Friendly's bar
I'll be drinkin' bottled water with just a twist of lime
And the cowboys that dance with me tonight are going to
    have a good old time.

Bridge
I know that you think I'm lonely, gonna window shop
Not this time, babe, this one-sided love must stop

Chorus Repeat

Urp, Slop, Bring the Mop

Verse
She's got him steppin' and glidin' cross the dancing floor
My friends and I can't take it anymore
He's got a smile on his face that's saccharine sweet
A hat on his head and boots on his feet

Chorus
Urp, slop, ohoo, bring the mop
Oh check out Johnny Ray Hickenboch
He's dressed in country clothes that she bought from Sears
Having fun without having a beer
He's drinking bottled water with a twist of lime
Doin' country dancing where they stand in line
Urp, slop, ohoo, bring the mop
Check out Johnny Ray Hickenboch

Spoken: Girls, look at that silly shirt, and his hat doesn't
    even fit

Verse
She's got him walking in the park and holding hands
To simple music with words he understands
Looking for a sunset in the middle of the day
Wearing matching shirts that read *s'il vous plait*

Chorus Repeat

Bridge
Music, sunsets, and holding hands
Sure sounds good to me
But I wonder what my friends would say
If they should happen to see

Chorus Repeat

Tag
Urp, slop, bring the mop
Oh man, check out Johnny Ray Hickenboch
I think I'm going to be sick

Chapter 9
Interdigitations

All day and into the night I prayed and prayed that Mrs. Knott wouldn't give me away. The next morning I made sure Ronny got on the bus first, just in case I needed to hightail it. Ronny jumped on.

"Good morning, Johnny Ray," she said. "Did you get up on the right side of the bed with your right foot forward today?"

"I'm pretty sure I did," he answered.

"I like your country shirt, Johnny Ray. Did you get that through the Sears, Roebucks catalog?"

"Yes, and it looks just like its picture." As he walked back to his seat, he pulled out his pen and pad.

"Come on, Tommy, get on," she said with a smile.

I forgot to 'start out right' that morning. I forgot my own new saying, but at least my prayers were answered. God made Mrs. Knott forget that I told her Ronny's real name.

The fifth grade turned out to be the best year of all my schooling. Yes, I had to read in front of the class the very first day. But that was the last time. The teacher, Miss Obakercher, moved me to desk number one, row one. My desktop actually touched the side of her desk. She said she was seating us by our size and/or reading ability. Even though I was a year older, I was still one of the smallest, and I was by far the worst reader. I guess it was easy to tell—she only made me try to read the first sentence of a paragraph. Regardless, there I was, looking like the teacher's pet. I remember reaching over and thumbing the corner pages of one of her books. Little did I know that a poem in that raggedy-looking book would become instrumental in changing my life.

Every morning when the school bell rang, I would line up with the fifth-graders outside on the left walkway facing the school. The sixth-graders lined up in the middle, closest to the steps where the principal stood at the top. One of the teachers would pull the flag up the pole with a rope. We all sang "The Star-Spangled Banner," said the "Pledge of Allegiance," and recited "The Lord's Prayer." After the principal's announcements, we would wait while the sixth-graders went into the building first.

Every time, I would get what Mom told me were "the blues." Holding my head down but with my eyes up, I watched them climb every step every day. It killed me. *That should be me,* I thought. I could sing all the words to our national anthem. I never forgot to say the new words 'under God,' after saying 'one nation.' I was the only one in the class who knew what *art, hallowed,* and *thy* meant in the prayer. That was because of Mom's Bible reading.

The one thing Mom couldn't explain to me was why we were asking God to "lead us not into temptation." All the preachers said the devil, not God, did the tempting so he could lead us to hell. My teacher couldn't even give me the answer as to why that line was in the prayer. I just knew I was as smart as a lot of those sixth-graders, even if they could read ten times better than I could.

I was in hopes that the light would turn on that year. Mom told me that my brain would pull the switch someday. Then the words would be so bright they'd jump off the page at me. If that happened, I was hoping that the principal would put me back up a grade. I really needed to prove that "lead us not into temptation" should be taken out of "The Lord's Prayer." I thought if I could do that, I'd be up in the sixth grade for sure. Most of the so-called blues would go away by the time we walked to class and I was secure at my desk.

After a few weeks of school had gone by, I was doing okay. Miss Obakercher, who went by Miss O, found time to work with me on my reading—ten minutes before the morning bell or five minutes during lunch or recess. Knowing I was missing the first part of recess made me read a little faster. Miss O noticed that, especially on square-dancing days. Music played from one of the big oak trees.

Spanish moss hid the speakers on the branches hanging across our brick street dance floor.

"Tommy, when you take time to focus on the word, you read better," she said. I didn't take time to focus—I focused fast and hard. I wanted to get out there and do-si-do with the girls.

One day during the silent reading time, I got a little bored. With the eraser end of my pencil, I lifted and dropped the cover on the old used book.

"Tommy," Miss O whispered with squinted eyes, "you know better. You're not to touch anything on my desk."

I whispered back, "Miss O, why do you keep this book on your desk? Do you ever read it anymore, or is it too old?"

"This is American literature at its finest," she said. She picked it up gently with both hands and held it to her chest.

"I don't like a lot of poetry," I said. "It's hard to understand. It's like they leave some words out or something."

"Do you have a favorite poet?" she asked.

"The only ones I know are from Peter, James, and John."

"I don't think they were poets, Tommy."

"They wrote part of the Bible, and Mom says that the Bible is pure poetry."

Miss O smiled.

"Is that true or is it just another saying," I asked.

"It sounds like it's true to your mom, Tommy," she said. "Students, clear your desktops. I'm going to read y'all some poetry."

"Can you read us a story instead of a poem," I asked. "Please."

Other students agreed with me.

"Most poetry is a story, like this one here, a love story between a man named . . ."

"Are there any cowboy stories in that book?" I asked.

"No, but I think you'll like this one. Edgar was in his mid-twenties. He had fallen in love with and married his fourteen-year-old cousin."

I figured they must have been fourth or fifth cousins, distant enough so they could be more than just kissing ones, like Ronny was with ours.

"No talking and no questions until I've finished the poem." Miss O started reading.

Annabel Lee
By Edgar Allan Poe

It was many and many a year ago,
  In a kingdom by the sea,
That a maiden there lived whom you may know
  By the name of Annabel Lee;
And this maiden she lived with no other thought
  Than to love and be loved by me.

I was a child and she was a child,
  In this kingdom by the sea,
But we loved with a love that was more than love—
  I and my Annabel Lee—
With a love that the winged seraphs of heaven
  Coveted her and me.

And this was the reason that, long ago,
  In this kingdom by the sea,
A wind blew out of a cloud, chilling
  My beautiful Annabel Lee;
So that her highborn kinsmen came
  And bore her away from me,
To shut her up in a sepulchre
  In this kingdom by the sea.

The angels, not half so happy in heaven,
  Went envying her and me—
Yes! —that was the reason (as all men know,
  In this kingdom by the sea)
That the wind came out of the cloud by night,
  Chilling and killing my Annabel Lee.

But our love it was stronger by far than the love
  Of those who were older than we—

Of many far wiser than we—
And neither the angels in heaven above
Nor the demons down under the sea
Can ever dissever my soul from the soul
Of the beautiful Annabel Lee;

For the moon never beams, without bring me dreams
Of the beautiful Annabel Lee;
And the stars never rise, but I feel the bright eyes
Of the beautiful Annabel Lee;
And so, all the night-tide, I lie down by the side
Of my darling—my darling—my life and my bride,
In her sepulchre there by the sea—
In her tomb by the sounding sea.

They "loved with a love that was more than love." Now, I didn't understand that line in the poem. If they cared for, respected, knew, and understood each other, it was love. No more, no less. It was like Bobby had explained to me: "Forever," he said, "was forever." So when the preacher said "forever and ever," he was wasting his breath on the second *ever*. *Amen* means to agree—no need to say it twice at the end of a prayer. So I felt that if they loved, they must have had Mom's four-ingredient recipe. That was all they needed; it was love.

We had an agreement. If we—especially me—behaved, Miss O would read and explain the love of Edgar and Annabel Lee. Every morning for the first fifteen minutes of class, I was transformed, watching and listening as I stood on a rough, rocky cliff. I was on the Northeastern coast near a place called Boston. A pathway weaved its way down the rugged terrain, through a plateau, and into the breaking waves of the Atlantic Ocean. On this small but heavily sanded plateau, just out of reach of the pounding surf, was a sepulchre. The moonbeams bounced over the salty sea, spraying some dim light onto the tomb of Annabel Lee.

I'd had a lot of experience with the graveyard thing at a very young age. "Miss O, no way would I lie where Edgar did every night, dream or no dream. Do you think Edgar could have cared for Annabel that much?"

"They cared for each other so much that they were coveted by the winged seraphs of heaven," she said.

"What's a seraph? I know that to covet is to want something that doesn't belong to you."

"Very good, Tommy. How do you know the definition of *covet*?"

"It's in the Bible. It's one of the Ten Commandments that my mom taught me."

"Well, seraphs are believed to be heavenly beings that have six wings. They live in the highest of heavens with God."

"So they are celestial bodies, then?" I asked.

"I would say that you're right again, Tommy. From the Bible, I presume?"

"My mom read that to me out of First Corinthians. But what does *presume* mean?"

Every morning for weeks, Miss O read "Annabel Lee." She controlled my thoughts from the beginning. Her voice of hopelessness filled the room before she completed the first line. At every reading her same facial expressions would come and go at the same spot. Her voice edged on scary by the middle of the first verse. It would convert to innocence by the beginning of the second.

Halfway through the third verse, I recognized the heavy sadness and knew the burning feeling that had to be down in her chest. I was sure it was even deeper down than a Bible-bosom feeling. It was the same feeling I'd had over Ronny, when he and Dad weren't getting along. I saw it in her watery eyes and heard it in her trembling voice. She sounded like she knew the people in the poem or was actually there in this "kingdom by the sea." It was as if she was trying to pick up the pieces of Edgar's broken heart. She spoke the fourth verse with pity and desperation. In the fifth verse she triumphed with inspired confidence, but she fell into an accepted fate in the last.

It was hard for me to believe, but the day came when the class voted against hearing "Annabel Lee"—mainly because of Billy Robinson, last row, last seat. He was the biggest kid in the fifth grade, maybe in the whole school. I wondered if Miss O had put him in the back of the room because he also had the biggest mouth. That was always a question in my mind. He was the big bully who always had something smart to say. He never let me, or others, forget that I was a flunky, older but smaller, bad reader, and didn't dress that cool. That was all true, but he couldn't find anything bad to say about my sneakers.

I rode the bus instead of walking that next morning. I wanted to see if Ronny had any ideas on how to keep Miss O reading "Annabel Lee." I sat down beside him. "Ronny, my teacher isn't reading my favorite poem every morning anymore," I said.

"Every morning is a little much anyway," he said.

"Well, it's because of Billy the bully asking for the class vote."

"Who does he bully?"

"Everybody and anybody," I said.

"Has he ever touched you?"

"He's tripped me from behind a couple of times."

"If you had tagged his nose on the first trip, there wouldn't have been a second," he said.

"He got me when I was feeling blue."

"Blue, my ass. You better get the 'Red Ass' and kick his ass till it turns blue."

I guessed that Ronny didn't believe in the "turn-the-other-cheek" Bible story. I knew Jesus had gotten angry with the money changers in the temple, so I figured I had a right to get angry with Billy. I was pretty sure that's what Ronny's getting the Red Ass meant. He gave me all kinds of advice that morning.

"He's big, so hit first. Hit the nose hard and put his lights out so he goes to sleep. Make sure a teacher is around to break it up in case you don't connect." We reached the junior high, and Ronny got off the bus.

"Hey," I yelled out the window. "Are the lights his eyes or his brain?"

He yelled back, "The nose is the button. It's a combination. I'll demonstrate on you when we get home tonight."

As soon as I had stepped off the bus, right in front of everyone, I heard smart-aleck Billy.

"Hey, Tommy, did your Mommy read you to sleep with a little bedtime Bible story?"

"As a matter of fact, she did."

"Figured, because we know you couldn't read it yourself," said the mouth.

Enough was enough. That was it, time to knock him out. I had been thinking and planning for our "come-to-Jesus meeting" long before I talked to Ronny. I wanted it to be at the end of the last day of school. If I'd gotten kicked out of school and failed two years in a row, it would have broken Mom's heart. I didn't know about my ass, but I knew my face was red. "Billy," I said, "what do say we go around—"

"Over here, Tommy," said Miss O. "We have twenty minutes before the bell. Let's go."

She placed her hand on my shoulder and directed me toward the classroom.

I remember keeping my eyes fixed on Billy, thinking that for a guy who could read, he wasn't very smart. He didn't know it, but losing a fight didn't matter to me at all. I had never won one. I'd been in a lot and had the bumps, scars, and missing hair to prove it. I'd been beaten in bunches, like radishes. Dad, Bobby, Ronny—all had taken turns on me, sometimes on the same day.

How big he was didn't matter. I was thinking I was due for a win. In a fight with him I would at least be hitting back. I never ever thought of exchanging punches with Dad. Bobby would hold me off with his long, wiry arm, letting me swing away at nothing but air. If I hit Ronny, he wouldn't stop or release me until right before I reached the veil of death.

I sat down at my desk, with Miss O at hers, and started to pull out my reading book.

"Tommy, wait a minute," she said. "Since we won't be reading 'Annabel Lee' anymore, I think you should have a copy."

"You do?"

"Yes. Now, Tommy, you will be the first student I have ever allowed to hold and have this book at their desk. I expect you to treat it—"

"I will treat it like my family Bible," I said. And I did.

During the silent reading time, I would write, read, live, and breathe the story of Annabel Lee. Every night I worked at enunciating, reading, and spelling each word. I practiced saying it just like Miss O. I did it over and over again, standing in front of the mirror. When Dad wasn't home, I would sneak Mildred in. She'd lie down and watch me the whole time. Every time I made a mistake, she would look up at me strangely and tilt her head to the left. I didn't know how she knew.

I would copy and recopy. I couldn't count the number of times I started and restarted. Miss O let me use as much paper as I needed. She even moved the wastepaper can over to my side of her desk. I wanted the copy of "Annabel Lee" to be in ink. I was also trying to make it look as pretty as my sister Norma's writing. I had gotten to the last verse a couple times before screwing it up. I made it over halfway many times. Then Miss O would point out a mistake in an earlier verse.

Finally, by the last week of school, I knew and understood every word. I never completed a copy in ink. I did in pencil, though, with only one dark eraser mark. That smudged mark was on the third to last word. I had put an *E* instead of an *A*. I had misspelled the very name of the man whose writings changed my life. "AproPoe," I presume.

The last day of school came. It was the first time that I didn't want to hear the final bell ring. We'd had a little classroom party. Big mouth Billy Robinson was batting a thousand in helping me get the Red Ass.

"Okay, everyone, back in your seats with arms folded for the very last time this year. Tommy, please stand in front of my desk and face the class. Students, may I have your undivided attention for a special reading by Tommy Brooks of 'Annabel Lee,' by Edgar Allan Poe." She handed me the book with teary eyes and smiled.

I turned to the poem and stood there staring at the page. I

heard a snicker from the back row.

Miss O leaned up over her desk behind me. "You are not Tommy, you are Edgar in this kingdom by the sea. Not only do you know it by heart, you feel it in your heart. Now, read and let them feel it. Make them feel the 'love that was more than love' with you and your Annabel Lee."

The words of Edgar started flowing as I pictured myself lying next to the sepulchre by the sea—where I said I would never lie. Yet now, I felt like I truly belonged there. I felt the unwanted but accepted fate as I uttered the last line: "In her tomb by the sounding sea." For a few seconds, I thought I could actually hear the sounding sea. I looked up. The sound I heard was that of the whole class standing and clapping.

"Tommy, you gave it by heart, eyes closed, without missing a word," said Miss O. "You gave every line with feeling, emotion, and conviction." She and the class continued to clap.

The bell rang. Miss O leaned over and whispered in my ear, "Tommy Brooks, lover of Annabel Lee, you were my favorite student."

I had to get out before I started to cry. I made my way to the middle of the class and out the door. Everyone was saying, "See you next school year. Have a nice summer." With my head down and walking fast, I got out the front doors of the school. Partway down the wide cement stairs, something told me I had to go back and say something. I had almost made it back to the top when I went down. I tripped from a hard push that sent me stumbling on the stairs on my hands and knees. My pants were torn, and my knee was bleeding—not that bad, but the rubber on the toe of my left All Star was scuffed up. I got back on my feet to the sound of laughter and singing.

"School's out, school's out. The teacher let her little pet monkey out."

There was the mouthy bully standing two steps below me. It put his nose right at my shoulder level.

I was already sad. Now I was mad.

"Is it okay with you if I check something out that my brother told me," I asked.

"Remember, Miss O, which stands for Miss Zero, is not around anymore to protect—"

Bam! I hit that button nose so hard his lights had to at least blink. I didn't know if he was surprised, stunned, or both when I helped him sit down on the step. After that I decided I best not go back inside. I went back down the stairs and across the front of the school. There was Miss O leaning out our first-floor classroom window.

"Hey, Tommy, come over here," she said. "You didn't say goodbye to me."

I wanted to say everything but goodbye. I wanted to say that I loved her, but I couldn't say that to a teacher. Anyway, Mom told me she was the only girl that I was allowed to love. I could tell her I wanted her to be my teacher next year. Then I could get to know and understand her better. If I could tell her how much I cared for or respected her, she would know it meant the same as love. I really needed to say something, but I couldn't find the right words.

There I was, only a foot below the window, one-on-one again with Miss O. She had gotten on her knees, folded her arms on the windowsill, and rested her chin on her hands. I stood with my sore left hand in my pocket and the fingers of my right hand propped across my lips.

"Weren't you going to tell me goodbye?" she asked.

"No." Then I softly mumbled, "I just wanted to tell you thanks."

Then it hit me. Just like playing a reverse run in football at recess, I would tell her in reverse. I would tell her how she felt and what she had done for me instead of how I felt toward her.

"Tommy, take your hand away from your mouth and look into my eyes."

I put my hands behind my back, holding the throbbing left hand with my right.

"Now, using your Edgar voice, tell me what you have to say, like, 'Goodbye, have a nice vacation . . .'"

"Edgar tells it from the heart, broken or not," I said.

Her smile broke out and up into her ruby-red cheeks. "That's even better. Edgar, tell me what Tommy wants to say from way down in his heart."

This time I kept my eyes open and looked into hers as she had asked. "Thank you, Miss Obakercher. Thank you for being my teacher. Thank you for caring that I can't read very well. Thank you for caring enough to give up your free time for me. Thank you for respecting me enough to trust me with your favorite book. Thank you for knowing how to make me feel important. Thank you for knowing that I needed to sit by you. Thank you for knowing that I needed to fall in love with Annabel Lee. Thank you, Miss O, thank you for respecting me, for knowing me, and for caring for me. Thank you for understanding."

Miss O's smile was gone. She had her glasses off and dabbed her eyes with a flowered hanky. "Tommy, where and when did you learn to say such nice, grown-up words?" she asked.

"I learned them in the car on the move here from Cincinnati," I said. "My mom taught me that those are the words that make up love. I memorized them over this past school year, but this is the first time I got to use them."

"Well, I love you too, Tommy. No one has ever told me thank you so many times."

"My mom said that *thank you* are the two most important words in the English language."

"Really?"

"Yeah, she said they had to be, because the world spends millions of dollars each year to put them at the end of telegrams."

"Well, Tommy, thank you too. I will never forget you, Tommy Brooks." She got up off her knees and slowly started closing the window, stopping a couple of times to blow her nose. "So long now, Tommy. Make sure you practice your reading this summer."

I walked backward, waving goodbye.

She waved back as she disappeared from the window.

As I turned around and slowly started walking away, I heard, "Let's move it. Get the lead out . . ."

It was Ronny yelling and knocking off his newfound cowboy hat getting into the backseat of the car. The hat was made of straw, with the front brim bent down over his eyes. He wasn't fooling me. He used it to hide behind when needed. Dad had picked Bobby and Ronny up from school too. We were going to an end-of-the-school-year fish fry at the Elks Club. I wondered if the Elks would get mad. Dad still wore his ring from the Masons.

"Come on, Tommy, you can get in the front," Dad said.

I wiped my eyes on my shoulders and pulled the door closed with my right hand, leaning over on the seat with my left. *Wow, that hurt.* I quickly pulled my limp hand back and into my lap.

"What happened to your hand," Dad asked. "Why is it so swollen?"

Ronny threw himself forward, hanging over the seat, and reached for my hand. "Let me see," he said. "Did you do a little interdigitation and pop the bully in the nose?"

"That word means his digits," Bobby said. "In this case his fingers were interlocked. Hard to hit someone if the fingers are intertwined together."

"Did you get down and dirty, go to the ground and intertwangulate?" Ronny asked.

"No such word as *inter* . . . whatever," Bobby said. "Quit trying to be cool, making up new words. The word you're looking for is *wrestle*. Webster's Dictionary has already beaten you to it."

"Did you put his lights out?" Ronny asked.

"No, but I think I made them flicker a little," I said.

Miss O moved out of town that summer, and I never got to see her again. But Billy and I became the best of friends.

Interdigitations

Verse
I spent the morning with a shrink
Telling me what I think
He said I really couldn't see
Just what you needed from me
I went with tongue in cheek
I left on bended knees
Asking would he please
Explain you to me

Chorus
He said interdigitations before intertwangulate
You gotta hold 'em and hug 'em
Squeeze 'em and love 'em
Like you did on your first date
You got to have interdigitations before you intertwangulate

Verse
Those words went over my head
He took a pencil and pad
Began explaining to me
The difference in he's and she's
He said a thank-you and please
With a smile and a tease
Don't try to change what you see
Un, un, un just let her be

Chorus Repeat

Chapter 10
If Only From Heaven

My grandma passed away almost a year to the day that Grandpa died. It wasn't until a few weeks later, when Mom was cleaning out the kitchen cabinets, that it hit me. I was on the porch in the rocking chair looking up at the sky. I was missing Grandma and wondering if she could see me from heaven. Then I heard Mom.

"I can't tell if these Mason jars of guava jelly are still good."

"Mom, did you say guava?" I asked.

"Yes."

I couldn't help it. I started laughing and crying at the same time. Just then a light rain began falling over the guava trees, with the sun still shining. That was my answer. Grandma could see me, and she was smiling and crying too.

The rain stopped as fast as it started. I got up, went into the kitchen, and made myself a peanut butter and guava jelly sandwich.

"Tommy, do you like that jelly?" Mom asked.

"Well, I've developed a taste for it," I said.

"What do you mean you've *developed*?"

"Oh, a little taste here and a little taste there."

"Really," Mom questioned, surprised.

"Yeah, fruits are like people. If you give them a chance, you just may learn to love them."

"Who did you hear that from?" she asked.

"From someone I learned to love."

Over that next couple of years I did a lot of hunting and fishing. My older cousin let me tag along with him. He showed me how to skin gators, catfish, and snakes. I learned how to set out trout lines on the Saint Johns River and hide from the game warden at the same time. The killing of gators and snakes and catching fish didn't bother me, but using dogs to tree a raccoon and shoot it down wasn't fun for me. It didn't take a great shot to knock a helpless animal out of the top of a tree. After all, how many raccoon-skin hats did we need? If you ran the dogs, and they picked up the scent, they'd smell out and tree the coon. The fight was over, or at least it should have been.

The fight didn't stop for me either. It was easy getting tougher, braver, and stronger over that time. My plan of watching, listening, and copying worked on the water, in the woods, and in the swamp. I had learned a lot over those two years, but nothing that helped me with school. I received forty-five licks from the assistant principal my first year in the seventh grade. The second year, I managed to reduce that to thirty-five. It had gotten to the point that even I knew the fighting and misbehaving was out of hand.

The principal called me into his office again. "Tommy, I know you don't want me to phone your parents, do you?"

"No, sir, please don't," I said.

"Well, I tell you what. For the next two weeks you come and see me before the bell rings. We'll give you three good swats every morning. Maybe that will help you get through the day without fighting and acting up in class."

"Thank you," I said. "I think that will work."

"Good," he said, "then we might as well get started today."

I put my hands in their familiar spot on the edge of his desk and locked out my elbows. I bent at the waist and spread my legs to shoulder width, as always. The principal sat across the desk in his old leather high-back chair and made me look him in the face. The assistant principal then delivered the message from the aerodynamic, hole-riddled paddle, appropriately named "The Messenger."

I had figured out many licks ago why the principal made me look at him. If he didn't see a tear, he tapped his pencil on his desk and the assistant principal brought the message faster, harder, and louder. I did everything I could to keep him from having the pleasure of seeing me cry. I was more like Ronny than I thought.

The morning rendezvous must have worked—there were

no more fights, and it was a lot quieter in class. It seemed like I understood the half-inch plywood communication the best. The Messenger, however, didn't reach the fight going on inside of me. There I was, going on fourteen, finishing up my second year in the seventh grade. All my friends were one and two years ahead of me. It didn't matter that I was pretty good at sports. I wasn't allowed to play because of grades. My mom had even found an ex-schoolteacher to help me with my reading. It had been three hours a week for that past year of reading one word at a time. The ability to point my finger under each word even got slower.

Bobby's labeling of people started making sense. I found myself living in his category of sympathy. One night I overheard my mom and dad lying in bed talking, saying that they hoped I could learn my numbers and how to read a little better. If I did, maybe I could learn to manage a gas station someday. I had nothing going on in my life to be enthusiastic about. I couldn't even keep a girlfriend, I was so dumb. I was living in sympathy with no one around feeling sorry for me but me.

My dad was thinking of moving us to a farm out in Pedro, somewhere between Ocala and Wildwood, Florida. It was out in the country, thirteen miles from the nearest blinking caution light. I didn't care. I thought that maybe I could become a farmer if the gas station job didn't pan out.

I had given up and wasn't going to practice reading anymore because no matter how hard I concentrated, it didn't get any better. I got home after that last day of my finger-pointing reading session and sailed the book up and onto the roof of the house.

Bobby was sitting out on the porch reading the newspaper. "Are you mad?" he asked. "Do I sense a little anger?"

"No, I'm relieved," I answered.

"Are you sad and feeling sorry for yourself?" he persisted.

"No, I just don't care anymore."

"So you're saying that apathy has taken over your spiritual and physical being?"

"What about the apathetical smell of your ass with no concern for those around you?" Ronny yelled out from the kitchen.

"Shut up in there, you little hood," Bobby yelled back, "and just keep writing love poems to yourself, or whatever you're doing." He turned to me. "Why don't you practice by reading the paper?"

"I can't read that fourth-grade book on top of the roof. How am I supposed to read the paper?"

"Read it one word at a time," he said, as he pitched his pocket dictionary at me. "If you don't know it, look it up."

"One word at a time doesn't work. Whaddya think I've been doing? Since you know everything, tell me why my eyes roll or go up and down when I try to read."

"Due to the pending factors and vicissitudes of everyday life, I find myself incapacitated to comprehend your linguistic expressions," Bobby replied.

Ronny pushed open the kitchen screen door, letting it slam behind him. "What the hell is that? Why can't you just say you don't know? He asked you a simple question, and you have to answer with all that crap."

Bobby shook his head, and with a smirk, jumped off the porch. He walked off around the side of the house whistling the tune of "Oh! Susanna."

"Don't worry about it, Tommy," Ronny said. "He's just an ass."

I wasn't worried about it—I was amazed by it. I'd never known anyone else who talked or used those kinds of words. I was sure Bobby hadn't either. He had to have learned those words from reading. Maybe he found them in this little pocket dictionary. He must have made that sentence up from scratch. No way had he learned those words from using my plan of only watching, listening, and copying.

"Ronny, I need something to write with, quickly," I said.

He pulled his pencil off his ear and a piece of paper from his back pocket. He tossed them to me and walked back into the house. I caught the pencil, but the paper fluttered to the grown. I knelt down in the sandy grass, picked up the paper, and used the edge of the porch for a desk. I managed to look up the spelling and definitions for *pending* and *factors* in Bobby's dictionary and wrote down *Do to the . . .* It was late afternoon, and at that time, the pending factors were the awaiting mosquitoes around my head. The dive-bomber buzzing made me forget the next word that started with a *V*.

I got up, went into the house, and sat down at the kitchen table next to Ronny. Ready to go with pencil in hand, I asked, "Ronny, what was the word that Bobby said to me that began with a *V*?"

"Venereal."

"That's not it."

"Well, it should have been because that's what he was spitting out."

"No, really, it started out with a *vis* sound."

"Let me see what you're trying to write," he said. He turned my paper so he could read what I had on it. "Why do you want to write that down?"

"That sentence is the coolest. Bobby pulled all those big words 'right out of the clear blue,' as Mom would say. Then he put them into an answer to my question quicker than snot. I want to learn those words and be able to talk like that."

"*Incapacitated,* which is another word for *unable,* is the only word you need to learn from that sentence," he said. He pushed my paper back around. "You should start by spelling the first word of this, the *coolest* sentence, right."

"It's spelled right. The first word out of Bobby's mouth was *do.*"

"No, it was *due,* spelled *D-U-E.*"

"Just admit you don't know what the *V* word is either."

"I don't know," he said.

"Then don't try to make me think I'm that stupid. I know how to spell *do.*"

"I know you do, but you don't know how to spell *due.*"

"I know you're full of doo-doo,'" I said.

"Just so you know, there's another word with the same sound. It's spelled *D-E-W,* and it's from the moisture in the morning."

"Right, Ronny, if only the *D-O, D-U-E, D-E-W,* or doo-doo from heaven would fall and land on your head."

"You have Bobby's dictionary right there. Look it up."

I did, and Ronny was right. I wondered why the Webster guy would have ever needed to use *due to* the pending, when *because of* the pending worked just fine.

I wasn't going to get frustrated. So what that it was another sound-the-same, spelled-different, meaning-something-else word? I didn't care. I wanted to be smart enough to say that sentence to someone, someday. There I was, right back to my watch, listen, and copy plan. I had only a week left to get Bobby to help me. He was leaving to go out West for college. I didn't know why. He was already plenty smart.

~~~

I caught him sitting out front under the oak tree. He was in Grandpa's old iron-rusted, shell-looking rocking chair. The big thing was that he wasn't looking at a book or reading the newspaper.

"Hey, Bobby, what was that *V* word you said yesterday? The one when I was asking you about my eyeballs jumping and rolling?"

"Why?"

"Because I want to know. I looked up *pending* and *factors*."

"Then look up *vicissitudes*."

"How do you spell that?"

"I don't. You sound it out, write it down, and look it up."

"It would be a lot easier if you just spelled it out and told me what it means."

"It sure would be," he said. "Now get lost and come back when you know, and then I'll help you with the rest."

As fast as I could, I took out Ronny's pencil and paper. I said the word over and over, trying to figure out the spelling. I had come up with *vis-sis-a-tudes*. It wasn't in Bobby's little dictionary. I remembered going to the public library on a field trip back in grammar school. There was a huge dictionary at least six inches thick. It was sitting on what looked like a preacher's pulpit. My sixth-grade teacher had said that every word we'd ever need to know was in that book.
~~~

I took off walking down Mellonville Avenue and caught a ride in the back of a neighbor's pickup truck. He took me to the corner of Fifth and Oak. I was able to jump right out and run up the pathway to the library.

Just as I got to the big wooden doors, a lady on her way out grabbed me by the arm. "Slow down and keep quiet in there," she said.

"I haven't made any noise," I protested.

"Make sure you don't."

The door closed behind me before I could ask her if she thought she was the boss of the library.

Only the first two chairs of the otherwise empty long, dark wooden table were taken. There sat the two smartest girls from my first year in the seventh grade. School was out for the summer. I wondered why they were in the library and not at the lake or the beach. They started giggling when they saw me.

"Hi, Tommy," Linda whispered.

"What's so funny?" I asked.

"We didn't know you knew where the library was," she said.

"Well, it's right here. I walk past it all the time."

"We know you walk past it," Judy said. "Why are you in it?"

She was the one with the thick, continuous eyebrow.

"I need to use the big dictionary to look up a word," I explained.

As I walked on past them, Linda whispered a little louder so I'd be sure to hear. "Judy, why don't you go help him look up the word *cat* or *dog,* whichever one it is?"

They both laughed with their hands over their mouths.

The dictionary was in the same place but looked a lot bigger. It was hard for me to believe there were thousands of pages of words. In the *V-I-S* pages, the only words I recognized were *visible* and *visit.* No word was even close to *vis-sis-a-tudes.* I even looked through the *V-E-S* pages too, with no luck. I had started thinking that Bobby had probably just made the word up.

On the way out I was looking down at my paper so I

wouldn't have to talk to the girls, when I heard, "Young man, come over here, please."

I looked up. It was the lady who had told me to slow down and keep quiet. She was standing behind the circulation desk with a badge that read *Head Librarian.* I guess she *was* the boss.

"What's your name?"

"Tommy," I said.

"How can I help you?" she asked. "You've been looking for a long time in the dictionary. Let me see your paper. What word are you looking for?" She reached down over the desk and took the paper out of my hand.

"It's not a real word, or maybe I have it spelled wrong."

She looked at the paper and smiled. "Go back and look under *V-I-C.*"

"No, I know it's not a *vic* sound like in *victory,*" I said.

"Well, the *sis* sound you're hearing is coming from *C-I-S,* not *S-I-S* as in *sister.* This *A* you have in here is most likely an *I,*" she said.

"Okay, thanks a lot," I said. "I'll look it up some other day."

"Your real name is Thomas, right?" she asked.

"Yes, it really is," I said.

"Another young man named Thomas Jefferson said, 'Don't put off till tomorrow what you can do today.'"

I told myself I'd try it one last time. Of course I had to walk past the girls again.

"Did the librarian have to help you spell your hard word?" Linda asked.

"Yeah, I think I had a couple of the letters turned around."

"Did you get the letters of *dog* mixed in with *cat*?" Judy asked, almost falling out of her chair from laughing.

I didn't bother answering. I wanted to take one more look for the word and also test this Thomas Jefferson's saying. I turned to the *V-I-C* pages, and there it was. It jumped right off the page at me. The librarian was right. The *C* took the place of the *S,* and there was an *S-I* instead of an *S-A.* I remember standing there happy and proud as I wrote down the spelling and definition. *Vi-cis-si-tudes—unpredictable changes in life; ups and downs.*

I wondered how Bobby ever thought to look for it and how he was able to find it and use it. I could hardly wait to get back to the house to tell him what I knew. But I needed to get it into my sentence while it was still fresh.

I sat down at the table, three chairs from my smart, used-to-be classmates. "Linda, can I borrow a clean piece of paper?" I asked.

"We'll be going to high school next year, and you'll still be in junior high," she said. "Since we'll never see you in school, I'll just let you have a sheet instead of you borrowing one. By the way, did you pass the seventh grade your second time around?"

"Just a minute," I said. "Let me write this down before I get it mixed up."

Judy giggled. "Go ahead. We wouldn't want you to get *bowwow* mixed up with *meow*."

I finished up. I had at least half of the sentence and its translation down. "Yeah, I lucked out and passed this year," I said.

"Why didn't you just do it right and pass the first time?" snooty Judy asked.

I shrugged my shoulders up to my ears, leaned my head to the left, and said, "I don't know."

"You should know why by now," Linda said. "You just finished taking all the same classes over and some with the same teachers."

I almost answered that it wasn't the first time. Feeling a little embarrassed, I dropped my head and looked down at my paper. Then it hit me that it was time to practice. "I know the reasons why," I said, "but you probably wouldn't understand them."

"Tell us your excuses, so we can give it a try," Judy whispered, with her smart attitude and her eyebrow riding high.

"It was due to the pending factors and vicissitudes of everyday life, that's why. Well, I have to go. See you around, and thanks for the paper." I started toward the doors.

"Vicis-a what?" Judy whispered, a little too loud.

"Vicissitudes," I said.

"How do you spell it?" Judy asked.

"I don't. Write it down. Look it up. It starts with *V-I-C*, not *V-I-S*," I said.

Right as I hit the door, I heard a big "Shhhh, hush up over there." It came from the lady who gave me that great saying. I stopped and went over to the circulation desk.

"Is that you making all that talk over there?" she asked.

"No, the girls are having trouble with the spelling of a hard word. I just wanted to thank you for telling me the 'don't-put-off-till-tomorrow' saying. With all the unpredictable changes in my life, I would have quit looking."

She gave a little smile. Not too much, so as not to break the cake makeup on her face.

"You're welcome. It definitely sounds like you've found what you were looking for. Now, find the door quietly so as to not bother the girls again."

"I do have to go. I have some pending factors to take care of."

If Only From Heaven

If only the dew from heaven would fall
And light in your morning hair
And place back the shine of life once again
With that feeling of love that we share

If only the stars from heaven could see
And put back the beam in your eyes
That twinkle and gleam, that sparkle of light
With the feeling of love that we shared

If only the moon from heaven would glow
And put back the smile on your face
And replace the words to a soft gentle voice
With that feeling of love that we shared

I'm asking the dew, the stars and the moon
If one more day in your life they could spare
Because I just can't bear to watch you slip away
Without feeling the love that we've shared

Chapter 11
Smiling for No Reason at All

My "pending factors," meaning "awaiting circumstances," equaled zero. It didn't matter that I had nothing going on. In the last five minutes, I had made three sentences using only half of Bobby's coolest sentence. I stood outside, leaning back against the big brass handles on the doors, feeling the outline of my fifty-cent piece in my pocket. I had earned it from cutting old man Smitty's lawn with his push mower. Mom said I should have done it for free, but he made me take the money. I was feeling so tall and so smart, I figured I deserved a treat. I also wanted to see if I could come up with any more new sentences.

I zigzagged down the pathway and headed over to the drugstore on Main Street. Along the way I tried to decide what kind of milkshake I would get. *Or,* I thought, *I might get some French fries or a burger and a drink instead.* Standing off to the side of the entry was an old colored man who called me over. I asked what he wanted.

He opened his rough, callused hand filled with pennies, nickels, and dimes. "Young man, would you go in and get me a chocolate malt?" he asked.

"Sure," I said.

"You pick out what ya need and take yourself a dime or two," he said.

I did, and chocolate sounded pretty good to me too. I went in and came out with two chocolate malted milkshakes.

Another colored man, this one younger, came up and asked if I would do the same for him. He said he would like a vanilla one.

The first colored man bent over and opened his hand again. "Here, I'll pay for my son too."

A few coins had dropped, bouncing on the sidewalk. I quickly picked them up for him and pulled the rest of the needed change caught between his not-so-nimble fingers. I turned to go back in, and there was the soda jerk.

He stood with arms folded and his legs spread in front of the doors. "What are you doing?" he asked.

"They can't go into the drugstore, so I'm going in and getting them what they want," I said.

"That's not allowed. Y'all boys move on."

"Wait a minute," I called after the men. "Here, take my shake. It's not the kind you wanted, but I'm sure you'll like it."

The man took the shake with an unsteady hand and said, "Thank ya, young sir."

It was over that quickly. They both walked off toward Sanford Avenue. They didn't get to choose. They were lucky to even get something they didn't really want. It didn't make sense.

I went back in, sat down at the busy counter, and ordered a Cherry Coke. I sipped slowly on the straw, trying to think of some way to use my new words. I wanted to tell the jerk—who was a jerk in more ways than one—that he was wrong, but in a safe way. I didn't care that he was older or bigger and could throw me out—but I didn't want to be kicked out of the drugstore forever. By using the cooler words, I thought I'd be able to tell him off, without getting in trouble. He had stayed down working the other end of the counter, so it didn't matter that I couldn't think of anything to say that wouldn't lead to a fight or at least an argument. On the walk home I was hoping that the other half of Bobby's sentence had the words I needed.

That next morning was a Saturday, and Bobby was trying to sleep in. He had graduated and had been working for Dad toting garbage to get some money saved up for college.

It was still kind of early when I had asked him, "Are you awake yet?" I didn't get an answer or any reaction, so I said, "Vicissitudes are unpredictable changes. They are the ups and downs of everyday life."

"You're right," he said. "If I have to get up, you're going down. There will be some very predictable changes if you don't get out of this room. One will be the rearrangement of that big, dumb head of yours when I crack it open."

"You told me you would help me with the rest of the sentence if I learned the meaning."

"If you keep it quiet out there and wake me at noon, I'll do it. Now get out and close the door."

Dad had taken Mom to the store, and I knew they'd be back soon. Dad never let anyone sleep late. They returned at around eleven o clock.

Dad went in and pulled the sheet off Bobby. "If you sleep late you're cheating yourself out of life and the best part of the day. Now get up. You're leaving for school in a few days. You'll have to learn how to get up on your own. Your mother and I won't be there to baby you." Dad walked out of the room, and I walked in.

"Why didn't you wake me, so I wouldn't have had to listen to that?"

"You told me to keep it quiet and not to wake you till noon. That's almost another hour."

"Oh Lord," Bobby said, as he sat up on the side of the bed, rubbing his eyes with the heels of his hands. "Tommy, sometimes I wonder how you make it through the day."

"I did great yesterday, up until the drugstore soda jerk."

"Did I hear you giving me a definition earlier?"

"That was me."

"Where did you find it?"

"I found it down at the public library in that big dictionary."

"It's a miracle you actually know where the library is."

"Sure I know where it is. A couple girls asked me the same thing yesterday. Everyone in town knows where it is."

"How many times have you been there?"

"I've been there twice now, once before on a field trip."

"Momma will be proud. Now, what do you want?"

"Let's go sit at the kitchen table because I'm going to need some writing room," I said.

We sat down, but Bobby sat where Grandma used to sit when she and I would talk. I asked him to move over just in case she was around and wanted to sit and listen.

"Are you both dumb and crazy? Give me the pencil and

paper. I don't want to be here all day while you try to write, spell, and talk about dead people."

"You never know. Her spirit could still be around. Remember, this is her house."

"Shut up and tell me what you want."

"Write down what you said after 'vicissitudes of everyday life,' and write it nice so I can tell each word."

Bobby wrote it down really fast. "Here, now don't ask me what the words mean. Go back to the library and look 'em up."

I looked at the paper. It read, *I find myself incapacitated to comprehend the material.*

Bobby got up, went over, opened the icebox, and drank water straight from the pitcher. He'd never have done that if Dad had been in the kitchen.

"*Material* wasn't the last word in the sentence. It was *linguige* or something," I said.

"Oh yeah," he said, as he put the empty pitcher back in the icebox and belched out "expressions."

"How do you spell the word right before that?"

"It's *L-I-N* . . . Just go ahead and have Grandma spell the rest of it for you."

"So you do believe in life after death like the preacher talked about last Sunday?"

"What I believe is that your linguistics is not strong enough to communicate your thoughts to wherever Grandma might be," he said.

After hearing Bobby say the word that one last time, I wrote down *linjestic.*

On Monday morning I took off for the library. I went straight to the librarian and showed her my word.

"I know it's probably spelled wrong, but I think it has something to do with language," I said.

"It has everything to do with language. This *J* should be a *G*, and the *E* should be a *U*, and you're missing one more letter."

"What is it?"

"Tommy, there have been no 'unpredictable changes' since you were here the other day. I'm sure you can find it in the same dictionary that's in the same place."

"Thank you. Hey, you remembered my name from the other day."

"Well, you were the only one in here with 'pending factors.' Did you take care of them?"

"I have a new one to take care of over at the drugstore, so I got to get moving."

I remember walking back to the dictionary wondering why everyone I knew who could spell wouldn't. I thought that if I could, I would have been showing off, spelling everything for everyone. Starting off with the right spelling sure would have saved me a lot of time.

About twenty minutes later I had found the words *linguistic* and *expressions*. Bobby had already given me their definitions in the last thing he said to me. He said that my "linguistics" or language was not strong enough—good enough, that is, to "express" or "communicate" my thoughts to Grandma. That was pretty tricky. It amazed me that Bobby was able to use any word or the definition of that word when talking.

I spent the rest of that morning memorizing. I had the completed sentence and the definition of each word, and I read them over and over again. I closed my eyes and said the sentences again and again in my mind. Three hours later I had learned that a vocabulary grew by multiples with the defining of each word.

As quiet as it was in the library, the big clock could be heard from over five blocks away, bonging out twelve noon. It was time, and this time I was the messenger. I had to figure out how to make sure the delivery was right on. I thought of baseball and how this sentence could be used offensively, and that if I used it right, like a walk-off home run, I would need no defensive words. I only had to wait for the right pitch from the soda jerk.

I got a little nervous walking through the drugstore and sitting down in the corner booth.

"You can't sit there," said one of the soda jerks. "It's for three or more customers. You can take a seat at the counter here, if you like." He had his back turned jerking a soda and couldn't tell who it was by looking through the mirror. He turned around and saw it was me. "Well, lookie here, it's the little coon lover. Sorry, not only do we not serve coloreds in here, we sure don't serve nigger lovers."

Wow, the ninth inning came quickly, and I swung verbally as hard as I could, loud and clear. "Due to the pending factors and vicissitudes of everyday life, I find myself incapacitated to comprehend your linguistic expressions."

"You have no clue what you're trying to say with all those big words, you little punk," said the smaller soda jerk. He was pulling empty milkshake glasses off the counter and placing them in a bin below.

"Oh yes, I do. Let me break it down for you. *Vicissitudes* are changes in people's lives that they have no control over. Like the colored man and his son that the big soda jerk here ran off the other day. *Incapacitated* is when someone is unable to comprehend or understand why the big one here used such hateful language to degrade another human being."

To degrade another human being—where did that come from? I wondered. It was great, but it threw me off. I must have heard it in church or something. I couldn't think of what I was going to say next. All I could come up with was one of Mom's sayings. "I've lost my train of thought."

"You've lost it all right," said the big jerk. I was striking out.

Another saying crossed my lips. "Let me put on my thinking cap."

"That's your problem, you don't think," the little jerk squealed.

Then I heard the voice. It was Ronny coming from around the aisle with a cigarillo hanging from between his lips. It bounced up and down, forming a cloud of smoke over his head as he talked in his pretend-gravelly voice. He would say the sound came from his diaphragm, but it was fake, straight from the throat.

"Sorry, I couldn't help but overhear," he said. "Can I finish explaining your sentence for them?"

"This little wannabe Sambo needs all the help he can get," said the big jerk.

"No, I got it now. For a minute there I drew a blank. All my studying, and I couldn't think of what came after 'Due to the . . .'"

"Tommy, you know you sometimes get definitions mixed up. Let me." He turned to face the soda jerks and moved in close to the counter. "The words he forgot were *pending factors*. When translated, that means for you to shit in your fairy little white hats and pull them down over your ears."

The aprons and fairy hats came off as they started walking toward the open end of the counter. I lucked out and was able to grab Ronny by the back of his belt. He had flicked his cigarillo, and it bounced off an empty stool, sending sparks to the floor.

He had one foot on the stool and was headed over the counter when I snagged him. "Come on," he said, in his strained, tough-nose voice, "let me kick your little white asses for all the colored folk over in Goldsboro."

He made that sound by clenching his back teeth together. At the same time he'd raise a stiff upper lip, squint his eyes, and wrinkle his nose like a pig. At best it was a poor James Cagney, movie-star, tough-guy impression.

I managed to get Ronny out of the store only because a lady in one of the booths said she was going out to get the police.

We stopped running when we saw that the cops weren't coming. The jerks stood out front waving for us to come back. I had managed to keep Ronny moving with his arm stretched back. He was giving them the finger right in front of everyone.

"Why are you smoking?" I asked.

"I almost got in a fight for you over your *coolest* sentence. I take the chance of getting my ass kicked, and that's what you want to know?"

"Yeah, didn't you listen to the bishop preacher at that Mormon church? He gave us a 'word to the wise—don't smoke or drink.'"

"Well, I figure he was only talking to you. After all,

you're the wise one. You've added a half-dozen plus new words to that overflowing pea brain of yours."

We headed south on Park Avenue off of First Street. Ronny was quiet until we reached Fifth and Park and he saw the First Baptist Church. "I can't believe it," he said. "The jerks could be wiping the floor with my butt right now, and you're giving me a Sunday school lesson."

"I shouldn't have had to repeat it; you were sitting in the pew right next to me."

"Tommy, you sit there with one of Dad's ties on, which are way too big for you, by the way. You have this look on your face as if you're this bright, eager little mind, just thirsting for knowledge. No matter what church we're in, you think everything the preacher says is the gospel truth."

"Well, they are preaching the gospel, and Mom said they're men of God, and God is truth."

We cut down Thirteenth and across Sanford Avenue to Celery before Ronny stopped sounding like Bobby and admitted he was wrong. "You know what, Tommy, you're right. I go because I have to. You go because you want to. Keep going, listening, and doing what they say. I was wrong."

"Were you wrong about the ties too?"

"No, they should stop at the waist, not below your pecker."

Going to church was what most everyone I knew did on Sunday. I didn't go because I was religious. True, I went because Dad made me, but I also liked the stories. I didn't have to read, worry about a test, or compete. I got to sit, listen, and let my imagination take over. Regardless if they were Sunday school teachers, Bible class instructors, or preachers from the pulpit, they were all telling stories. The stories at one church might have been a little different from the other, but they were still entertaining. If the speakers testified that what they had said was the truth, I was more likely to believe them.

On the *Perry Mason* TV show right before someone was going to tell their story, they had to swear to tell the truth. They had to tell the whole truth and nothing but the truth, so help them God. I wondered if the stories would have been as good if the preachers would have had to take the oath. Mom had told me the same Bible stories, but the characters always said and did more. Sometimes she even put me in the story.

Sometimes I would add my own lines like, "Then I pulled out my sword and cut off his zuzu."

She would say, "Oh, God forbid," and change the story.

~~~

Tommy, you can keep my dictionary, but you have to learn a new word every day. Knowledge is power. Remember to never let them see you licking your wounds, or they'll rub salt in them. Sorry for all the salt. See ya.

Those were Bobby's last words to me before he took off out West for college. He had written them on the side of a brown paper bag and laid it at the foot of my bed. I read it slowly, several times, before asking Mom to read it.

"What does he mean about being sorry for the salt?" I asked.

"It means he loves you," she said.

"Salt doesn't mean love."

"No, Tommy. It's his way of saying he's sorry for all the teasing, fighting, and picking . . ."

Ronny chimed in, "It's to let you know he was sorry for being such an ass for so many years."

"Ronny, don't you talk like that in this house," she yelled. "I'm telling your father when he gets home."

"You can tell him anything you want," he said on his way out the back kitchen door.

Mildred was doing her half crying, half barking that she always did when she needed something. I heard Ronny tell her to "stay" as he ran and jumped off the back porch. That wasn't like him to leave knowing she needed water. While I filled her bucket, Mom came out and sat down in the rocking chair. I could tell that she had been crying.

"Are you going to tell Dad on Ronny?"

"No," she said.

"Because you're the peacemaker, and you know there
~~~

would be trouble, right?"

"This is Ronny's way of handling Bobby's leaving," she said.

"Was Ronny up when he left?"

"Yes, they called each other a few pet names, and then they hugged each other and . . ." Mom started tearing up.

"Why didn't he wake me up to say goodbye? I could have hugged and called him a few names."

"Tommy, he had enough trouble just writing you the note."

"Was he crying a little?"

"Yes, he was."

"Do you think that means he was holding it in and crying really hard on the inside?"

"Not just crying but dying on the inside," she said.

Ronny came from around the side of the house. He stood there watching Mildred drink with her head half down in the bucket of water.

"Tommy, why are you smiling?" Mom asked. "Don't tell me you're smiling for no reason at all."

"I'm not breaking the law when smiling for no reason at all, am I?" I asked.

Ronny put his foot up on the porch, wrote something down, and went in the house.

"What did Dad do when he left?" I asked Mom.

"He gave Bobby fifty bucks and a new pair of tennis shoes, and told him to come back when he graduates."

I knew why I had smiled. That's when I realized that Bobby loved me. He never gave me a direct answer to a question. He never spelled a whole word for me unless I worked for it. If I wanted to know how to do something, he'd show me if there was no other way, but he never did it for me. He cared enough to say no. He put up with me coming back again and again, usually coming with the same question phrased a slightly different way. He knew my limitations and understood me. The big thing was that he respected me. He believed that I could, and probably would, figure things out on my own.

"So Mom, every time Bobby hit or called me a name, he

was really rubbing love in my wounds?"

"Well, you could say that, but I'm sure there were times when he 'loved you but just didn't like you.'"

"Is that saying true?"

"It's very true, Tommy."

"Whaddya know, Bobby and I have one of those 'love-hate relationships.'"

"No, you silly thing. I didn't say he hated you."

Well, I already hated Bobby not being around. There was no one to tell me how stupid I sounded, no one to analyze people for me. I even missed him saying the word *interesting* when I did something my way—or the wrong way, according to him.

Ronny graduated from high school but never went to his graduation. He continued to live at home that summer. He joined the National Guard and got a job working at a clothing store downtown.

Bobby's physical departure from the family had been much more acceptable than Ronny's emotional separation. He was still there in body but not in mind. He would answer if you asked him something, but his thoughts were somewhere else. Mom said he was "confused" and wasn't thinking clearly.

He and I were sitting at the kitchen table one afternoon, drinking lukewarm Kool-Aid. At least I was. The night before, he had put the tray back in the freezer with only two cubes left instead of refilling it with water, and I told Mom.

She said, "That was just pure laziness."

His mind was sure working clearly when he came up with the bright idea of putting both cubes in his glass. He was going to stir them around until his got cold and then put them in mine. No need to explain the size of the cubes when he finally dug them out with his fingers. Luckily, just before the sure-to-be-Kool-Aid fight started, we heard Dad yelling at Mildred. I couldn't understand the words, but Ronny was able to make them out.

"What did he say?" I asked.

Ronny pulled the jar from my hand and slid it slowly across the faded plastic table cover. He started in with his rhyming fake-drama voice. "Listen close, Tommy. The screen door will close itself with a slam into kitchen smell of jelly and jam. And on the back porch sits a wooden chair where you can rock in the fresh country air. You will hear those dreadful words."

With Ronny's poetic intro, there Dad stood in silhouette. The bright sun beamed through the screen behind him. "I'm afraid that old dog is sucking eggs," he said.

Ronny gulped his last sip, got up, and walked out of the kitchen.

Dad had moved out of the doorway. He walked over and leaned back against the sink. I could see then that he had his thumbs tucked in behind the neck straps of his bib overalls. That had become his new stance for verbal communication since we moved to Florida. There was no more police belt to put his thumbs behind. I couldn't believe that Ronny didn't realize the possible consequences. If he did, I sure couldn't understand his apparent unconcern. There was only one other person who loved Mildred as much as I did, and he had just walked away all cocky like.

I didn't get a chance to learn how smart the raccoons and possums were in Cincinnati, but I did in Sanford. They were really smart. They had the great ability to find a way into the henhouse or chicken pen. Once inside they would bite a small hole in the end of an egg and suck out the yolk, leaving the shell almost totally intact.

With his tightened fist pulling down on his bib straps, Dad said, "Tommy, Mildred's been a good . . ."

"Don't worry about it, Dad. I'll take care of it."

I knew how important the eggs and chickens were, and I knew how unimportant dogs became if they didn't do their job. I had another older cousin who lived out of town on Lake Mary. He had a bunch of hunting dogs that lived or died with the "three-strike rule." By the third hunt a dog had to run with the others. If it didn't go with the pack and just hung around the truck, it was shot or left in the woods or swamp to fend for itself. I believe at that time, it was an unwritten law, at least among the Florida boys. I knew of this heartless act, but I never had to witness it being carried out.

On one of the nighttime hunting trips, I asked my cousin why he didn't bring his newest dog, Black Jack, along.

He didn't answer, but his little brother did. "Black Jack got dumped off in Midway—Colored Town—after the last hunt."

"Why?" I asked.

"Because my brother said some colored family would take him in."

"Did Black Jack not run with the other dogs?"

"Nah," he replied, "and he got five tries, not just three like in baseball."

I was going to make sure that Mildred never had to hear the "three strikes, you're out," saying. I got up from the kitchen table and went back to the room where Ronny was lying face down on the bed.

"Why did you just 'peacock walk' out and not say anything? Don't you have any clue what Dad will do to Mildred if she keeps sucking eggs?"

"If he's got his mind made up, there's nothing you can do. Close the door on your way out."

"I'm not leaving."

"Yes, you are."

"Are you going to help me save Mildred or not?"

"Out," he ordered.

"Do you think we can make Dad understand that she's getting older and that losing a few eggs doesn't matter all that much?"

Ronny broke out in song with a Buddy Holly line. "That'll be the day-ay-ay when I die."

I left without closing the door and went straight to Mom. She was alone in the kitchen cooking up some snaps and crowders. The open pot was steaming, and she was sweating.

"Mom, is the saying, 'You can't teach old dogs new tricks' true?"

"I sure haven't been able to teach your father anything new," she said with a laugh.

Smiling for No Reason at All

Verse
I still walk down to the cafe
Take our table for two
Wave to your favorite waitress
Who still talks about you
I saw you yesterday with him
And asked her what she thought
About the way he's got you smiling
For no reason at all

Chorus
It's just killing me
Draining the life right out of me
No, it's not premeditated
But it's murder in the second degree
Somebody please make the police call
You're smiling for no reason at all

Verse
She took off her name tag and apron
Sat down in your chair
Held my hand, looked me in the eyes
Said honey, I've been there
That you're smiling from the inside out
He's not breaking the law
By the way he's got her smiling
For no reason at all

Chorus Repeat

Chapter 12
Me in Love with You

I wasn't going to let anything happen to Mildred. My sister may have brought her home, and Ronny may have taught her the tricks, but she was my friend. She was the sweetest, smartest dog in our neighborhood, probably in the whole world. At least to me she was. She could sit, speak, roll over, play dead, and I think she may have even been able to tell time. Back in the sixth grade, my last year of grammar school, Mildred would show up at the closing bell. She'd wait for me under the shade of the big oak tree at the bottom of the steps. She didn't come every day, but when she did, she was never more than fifteen minutes early and never late.

Sometimes we took the long way home and walked down along the bank of the Saint Johns River. That was one of the few times Mildred got a bath. Tired or not, no matter how many times I told her to "go fetch," she would jump in, swim after the stick, and bring it back. She was the example of true obedience, and that was my answer. I had Ronny's singing confirmation of his own death on the day Dad would change or understand. I had Mom's long-time experience and assurance that Dad was hard to teach. My best and only chance was trying to teach Mildred.

A few days had gone by when Dad informed me that Mildred was hanging around the chicken pen again.

"She's not doing anything," I said. "I'll get her."

"You better make sure that dog's not sucking eggs," he said. Then he backed up off the front lawn and drove away in his brand new company 1960 Ford Falcon Ranchero.

How things had changed. I wasn't worried about getting to ride in the new truck, like I was with the Pontiac some five years earlier. It had become all about the love of a dog, and my quest to save her.

My grandparents had always let the chickens roam the orchard. They believed the eggs and the chickens tasted better because they ate the "fallen-over, ripened fruit." I was sure that was the saying for *rotten*.

Mom said the chickens were allowed out because it was cheaper and easier. "Your grandpa had to use less corn feed," she said, "and if he skipped a day or so of feeding, they didn't die from hunger. That chicken pen was falling apart and becoming dilapidated long before your grandpa passed away."

"Mom, how do you spell . . . ? Never mind. I found it here in Bobby's little 'dic.' It starts with *D-I*, not *D-E*."

"Tommy, you do not abbreviate *dictionary*," she said.

"Mom, Bobby would have never said, 'The pen was falling apart' or repeat the word *dilapidated* since you had already used it—which I think is a really neat-sounding word, by the way."

"What would he have said?"

"Wait a second, what does *R-U-I-N*—never mind, I got it: *ruin*. He would have said, 'The chicken pen was falling into partial ruin,' giving you the accrual definition of the very word you used. That's why he sounds so smart." My wet finger licked through the well-used, marked-up pages. "He's been cheating all this time with this little pocket dictionary."

Mom chuckled and shook her head. "You're kidding, right?"

The educational routine began that very morning. School was in session. I put a rope around Mildred's neck and led her down to the end of the grove near the chicken pen. I led her around to a half-dozen nests, letting her smell the eggs. Every time she would go to lick, bite, or roll the egg with her nose, I'd smack her jaw. When she would cower down and look up at me with surprise, I'd point my finger at her and yell, "No, you're a bad dog!"

After an hour and a dozen attempted egg bites, sniffs, and slaps, class was over. I took the rope off her neck, and she crept underneath the house. For protection, she got right below where Mom was rocking. Ronny had been sitting by the screen door, watching. Mom was looking at the newspaper but reading my mind. I sat down at the end of the porch with my back to her. Even so, she could tell I didn't feel good about my new dog-training school.

It wasn't long before Mildred began licking my feet from under the porch.

"Stop it, Mildred. I'm in love with you, but you're only making love to me."

"Tommy, what did you say?" Ronny asked.

"What's it to ya?" I said.

He stood up, leaned against the house, and wrote on his pad.

"Tommy," Mom said, "it's not easy to give such harsh but necessary correction to someone or something you love."

I needed to get the next line out before the tears came and my voice changed. "Mom, do you think Mildred will ever like or trust me again?"

"Tommy, God gave dogs the great ability to forgive and forget. Otherwise, they would have never stayed around long enough to become man's best friend."

"Really? Is that the truth, Mom?"

"Yes, and I've always wondered why the good Lord never gave that wonderful trait to us humans." Mom got up out of the rocking chair. "Here, use this folded-over newspaper when correcting Mildred. It's louder and scarier, but won't hurt her."

"Mom, do you think I can teach her to be obedient and not suck eggs anymore?"

I was looking for a yes or no answer, but she sat back down. She lifted her arm with her finger, pointed to the sky, and said, "Once!" in a firm, high voice. Then she slowly lowered her arm to her lap, softened her voice, and let it fade with "upon a time." She did this with the telling of every Bible story.

Bobby had told me that he didn't know of any stories in the Bible that started with "once upon a time," and Ronny had told me that beginning was appropriate for fairy tales.

Regardless, Mom could always get my attention with that introduction because I knew a good story would follow.

"Once upon a time there were two cities, side by side, named Sodom and Gomorrah. God had sent in his apostles to teach, to educate, even to plead with the citizens to change their wicked ways."

"It's kind of like I'm trying to do with Mildred, right?"

"I think so," she said with a little smile. The porch board squeaked faintly with every backward rock as she continued. "The Lord told the prophet Abraham that he was going to send angels to destroy the cities because of their wickedness. Abraham had a nephew named Lot, who lived in Sodom. In an attempt to save him, Abraham made a deal, or I should say deals, with God . . ."

"I didn't know God made deals," I said.

"Well, he does in this story, and it doesn't work out too well for Lot and his family. Abraham reminded the Lord that he was a just God and surely wouldn't kill the righteous along with the wicked."

"So God forgets things too, and Abraham had to remind him?" I asked.

"No, of course not. He was informing God that he knew that he was fair and wouldn't kill the good with the bad. Abraham started out asking the Lord not to destroy Sodom if he could find fifty-five, or maybe fifty, righteous men. When Abraham realized that he might have started out too high, he continued to deal. The Lord allowed him to do so because he loved Abraham.

"The requested number continued to lower as the hunt for the worthy became more difficult: forty-five, forty, thirty-five, thirty. Finally Abraham asked if God would spare Sodom if he could find ten good men. He begged, and the Lord agreed, but Abraham could not even find one."

"I bet I could find fifty righteous men right here in Sanford," I said.

"Well, don't go making any deals with God on that. You just might lose. Now please, for heaven's sake, let me finish the story. Abraham convinced the Lord to at least allow him to get Lot and his family out of Sodom. The angels went to Lot's house and told him that the Lord had sent them to destroy the city. They gave Lot and his family specific instructions to leave and never look back. Lot's wife, however, did not obey. She made the mistake of looking back over her shoulder and was turned into a pillar of salt."

"You're kidding me!" I exclaimed. "Man, if angels came to my house and told me that, no way would I look back."

"That makes me feel good, to know that you would be obedient," Mom said, as she stood up.

"Is that the end of the story?" I asked. "What does it have to do with Mildred sucking eggs?"

"Tommy, sometimes we let things of the world become more important to us than we should. Mildred has developed a taste for eggs. We can only hope she doesn't love them so much that she's willing to suffer the consequences."

"But Lot's wife was a human, not a dog."

"Yes, but like so many of us humans, Lot's wife had fallen in love with her eggs."

I realized that Mom was attempting to give me another lesson in obedience. "Okay, Mom, so what eggs were so important that Lot's wife was willing to disobey God?"

"It could have been any number of eggs, Tommy." Mom held onto the doorknob. She looked into the house through the screen and continued with her explanation. "You could think that she was only reminiscing. In that one last moment, she tried to steal one more look at what she was leaving."

"Getting turned into a statue of salt for taking a little peek is playing kind of rough, don't ya think?"

"Tommy, only God truly knows the integrity of the heart. It wasn't the looking back. It was why Lot's wife looked back. Believe me, Lot's wife may have been the example, but she's not the only one. Many have disobeyed God because of their love for the material things of this world."

"I feel sorry for her, don't you?" I asked.

"I feel sorry that Lot's wife was unable to love the Lord more than her silver, fine linens, and silks."

"She had to leave her home and friends too," I said.

"I'm sure it was hard for Lot's wife as she turned around trying to grab a remnant of the past. In this case, grabbing an egg. And that's the end."

"Wait a minute," I said, "grab a remnant means like grab a piece or grab a part, right?" I asked.

"That's right."

"One last thing—aren't you glad you have a name so you don't have to be called "Jim's wife," all the time?"

~~~

Two months had gone by, and I had become hit and miss with Mildred's schooling. She had been staying close to the house and out of trouble, and I was sure my modified egg-sucking educational program had done the job. It was only a week later, after my private personal boasting, that things changed.

I came in the house hot and sweaty from playing football that Sunday afternoon. Right as the back side of my wet shorts and sticky thighs hit the plastic couch, I heard, "Tommy, you know you're not supposed to do that."

"I'm tired, Mom. I'll wipe it off when I get up."

"I'm talking about you jumping the fence and playing football in the stadium."

"You mean you're talking about us playing the Negroes?"

The stadium was the New York Giants' baseball training camp. In the off-season, it was the whites against the coloreds.

"Are you playing touch or tackle?" she asked.

"It always ends up tackle," I said.

"You wait and see. There's going to be a big old fight one of these days, and you're going to get hurt."

"Mom, kids have been sneaking in and playing against each other for years. I've never seen or heard of one fight. We're just having some fun playing ball against each other."

"You know there's still a lot of white folks around here who don't like that. I heard it wasn't too long ago that they booed that one colored player off that same field and out of town. It didn't even matter that he was supposed to be good."

"Mom, that was fifteen years ago. It was Jackie Robinson, and he wasn't good—he was great."
~~~

"Well, I worry about you. I'm also worried about your father. He's been down at the chicken pen since he got home."

"What's he doing?"

"Now, Tommy, I wasn't going to tell you. Remember, in the story where Lot's wife couldn't help grabbing a remnant of the—"

"Mom, what are you talking about? You're quoting scripture, giving me a lecture on football segregation, and Dad's out back with Mildred."

I exploded off the couch and across the living room through the kitchen, where I knocked over a chair and fell down myself. I managed to reach up and unlatch the screen door from my knees. By the time I crawled my way to the edge of the porch and stood, Mildred was at my side. I wasn't able to see Dad from the trees, but I heard the call.

"That's strike two!"

Someway I needed to figure out an advanced, more accelerated teaching program for Mildred. I talked Mom into giving up the full length of one of her only four clotheslines. Ronny tied a special choke-free Boy Scout knot in the rope around Mildred's neck and attached a free-sliding doughnut-looking one to the clothesline. That way she was able to still get under the porch for shade and water.

In my science class we had been learning about Pavlov's dogs. Bell rings, dogs get food, dogs get used to food coming when the bell rings. They salivate and eat. Pavlov rings the bell but doesn't give the food. The dogs still slobber in preparation for eating. Hence, conditioned response.

This was one of the few times I could remember trying to use something I'd learned in school, besides arithmetic at the store. The problem was I needed to use it in reverse. Give the food, in this case the egg, wait for the drooling, and ring Mildred's butt with the *Sanford Herald.* Instead of walking her down to the eggs, I brought them to her. At least an hour every day for weeks, I never missed. I placed eggs beside her and along her restricted, worn-out pathway. I would sit on the edge of the porch holding the folded newspaper. I watched, hoped, and prayed that that day would be the day Mildred would not touch an egg.

One late afternoon I was at my familiar teaching spot. I sat swinging my legs to a slow, sad song. I could barely hear it. It was coming from the neighbors' brand new pocket transistor radio.

Mom came out and sat down in her favorite storytelling spot and began to rock. "Tommy, you've had that poor dog tied up for a long time. That animal needs to be free to roam."

"But, Mom, if I set her free, she's going to suck eggs, and Dad will get rid of her."

"Son, you can take her freedom away, but you can't take her free agency."

"What's the difference?"

"Her freedom is only as long as the rope you have tied around her neck. Her free agency to want the taste of an egg can be endless. Tommy, try as you may, your desire to control her desires may be hopeless."

"Mom, I can't give up. I've got to get her to understand that if she'll obey me, she'll be okay."

"Would you like to hear a Bible story?"

"Sure, why not," I said. I looked back over my shoulder.

Mom had her arm up, finger to the sky, and as always, dropped it slowly to her lap. "Once upon a time, in a faraway land, there lived a smart, strong, rich man named Naaman. He was a great commander in the Syrian army."

"Was that his real name or did you make it up? Because *named* and *Naaman* rhyme."

"That was his name, and the king liked him very much. He had the best-looking chariot with the fastest horses in all of Syria."

"Where's that?"

"It's next to Israel where Jesus lived, and no, I don't know if they knew each other. Even with all his wealth, Naaman could not buy his freedom from the dreaded disease of leprosy. The skin of a leper—"

"I know what that is. Ronny and I saw *Ben-Hur* at the Movieland Drive-In last week."

"Where did you get the money?"

"We got in the trunk of—"

"Don't ever do that again. You could suffocate. Why does that Ronny teach you things like that?" She paused. "Okay, Tommy, let me finish telling the story without you interrupting."

"Are you adding things, or is this how the story really is in the Bible?"

"It's as close as I can remember."

"Do you know if Naaman had sharp-bladed hubcaps on his chariot like in the movie?" I wanted to know.

"I'm sure he did. After all, he was a warrior."

"You said he was a commander."

"He was captain, commander, warrior, and Indian chief. His chariot was red, with six pure-white horses."

"Great. Go on."

"During one of the battles with Israel, Naaman took a young girl captive. He gave her to his wife as a maidservant."

"Was she a good-looking chick?"

"The Bible doesn't—"

"Wait a second, Mom." I ran over, gave Mildred an assful of paper right as she licked an egg, came back, and sat down. "Okay, go ahead."

"One day this young girl asked Naaman's wife why he didn't go see the prophet of Israel and ask him to cure his leprosy. Naaman's wife told him what this very cute young servant had said."

"Sooo, she was a looker."

"Looks aren't everything, Tommy."

"No, but they're way ahead of whatever's in second place."

"Where'd you hear that?"

"Ronny," I said.

"Oh, Lordy. Well, anyway, Naaman told his king what he wished to do. The king told him that he should surely go. He even wrote a letter for Naaman to give to the king of Israel. It read, 'I have sent Naaman my servant, so that you might rid him of his leprosy. Thank you.' Naaman packed up his hot-rod-looking chariot with gold and silver."

"How much was there?" I asked.

"A whole bunch. That's why he had to have six horses instead of only four. It was going to be a gift for the man of God that could cleanse his rotting skin. That next morning he and his servants left their town of Damascus for Israel with great hope and the anticipation of receiving a miracle."

"Mom, do you believe in miracles?"

"Yes, of course I do, and I think I'm going to need one in order to complete this story. Okay, now. Days later Naaman reached the palace of the king of Israel and gave him the letter from his king of Syria. When the king read the letter, he got really mad and thought the king of Syria was trying to make a fool of him. He screamed that he was not God, that he could not kill and make alive. He told Naaman that his king knew that he couldn't cure him of leprosy.

"When the prophet Isaiah heard what had happened, he got word to the king of Israel asking him to send Naaman to him. Naaman and his servants took off for the prophet's house. They pulled up out front and slid to a dusty stop at the gate. Prophet Isaiah sent a messenger out telling Naaman to go wash in the River Jordan seven times, and he would be cleaned.

"Naaman jumped in his chariot, whipped his horses, and took off down the road with wheels spinning. 'I've traveled all this way,' he said. 'I thought this man of God would come out and wave his hands over me, removing my spots. But no, he sends out a servant to tell me to go wash in the dirty Jordan. We have two rivers in Damascus. They're bigger and far cleaner than all the water in Israel. I would surely come out cleaner washing there.'"

"Was that true, Mom? Was the water cleaner?"

"Tommy, it's not about the water. On their way back home to Damascus, they had to pass right by the River Jordan. The servants started talking to Naaman, saying, 'Master, if the prophet had asked you to do something hard, you would have found a way. But he asked you to do this one simple thing. You're here. Why do you not do it?'"

"Did he do it?" I asked.

"Well, freedom to do so was not a problem. He could get out of the chariot and walk into the water. No rope was holding him back. He also had his free agency to choose between the opposition. He could choose to obey the prophet or to ignore his own servants' wants and drive on."

"Did he dive in seven times and watch his dead, grody skin float down the river?"

"Yes, he was obedient. He washed seven times, and his skin became like a child's."

"That's a 'way-out' miracle isn't it, Mom?"

"Yes, it is, Tommy."

"I'm going to need one of those for Mildred, aren't I?"

Mom got up from the rocking chair. "Maybe you'll only need a little one, not a way-out one," she said, as the screen door closed behind her.

Mildred was able to go that whole next week without even smelling an egg during her Pavlov teaching courses. When I got home from school that Friday, she was lying on, not under, the porch. A couple feet of the chewed rope hung from her neck. Her tail wagged, thumping the porch on the downbeat. She had managed to gnaw her way to freedom. I was tired; she was happy and tired. I sat down and started petting her instead of scolding her.

I thought of a story my dad had told me once. When he was a young boy, a bird had found its way through a hole in the dining room screen. It made trips back and forth, bringing in twigs and grass and placing them on top of the armoire. I thought *armoire* was a really neat name for a cabinet. Dad said my grandpa even made the screen hole a little bigger for the bird and its building materials.

For days, Dad and Grandpa would watch the bird's clever placement and maneuvering of each branch. The day came when the eggs started to hatch, and Grandma told my dad that the nest, bird, and eggs had to go. Grandpa came in just as my dad was about to move the nest. He informed my dad that if he moved the nest, the mother bird would no longer care for her chicks. My dad asked Grandpa what he should do. Grandpa took my dad down from off the stool, looked into his eyes, and said, "Sometimes ya gotta know when ya just gotta let 'em be."

I stopped petting Mildred, held the hair back on her head, looked into her eyes, and said, "I guess it's time for me to just let ya be."

She dropped her head to the porch. She exhaled with a big sigh, and a puff of air flapped her lips. Maybe she was thinking miracle too.

Me in Love with You
(with you only making love to me)

Verse
I asked my dad just what he thought
About me loving you
He said it's okay
If you loved me too
You're looking nice and feeling good
Is not all it's about
Is the love that you give
Coming from the inside out?

Chorus
Because what lies ahead or lies behind
Is determined by what lies inside
If I could only see through you
What would I see
Me in love with you
With you only making love to me

Verse
I had a feeling down inside
What Daddy said was true
I wanted to ask my mom
Just what I should do
So I took that long and lonely ride
Out to her grave site
Swear I heard my momma say
Daddy's finally got it right

Chorus Repeat

Tag
Me in love with you
With you only making love to me

Chapter 13
Catch Me If You Can

Time went by. Mildred had been behaving, and I was doing a little better in school. I was sure it was because of those hours of holding Mildred's butt-smacking newspaper. During her resting time between the well-placed, tempting eggs, I practiced reading. The newspaper being typed in columns with shorter sentences is what I think really helped. I continued to practice reading the sports page. The front-page Southeast Asia stuff was boring and a lot harder to read. Besides, with the sports I could also practice math by refiguring the batting percentages.

A few weeks had gone by, and Ronny and I sat at the kitchen table wishing we had some of Grandma's guava jelly left. We wanted to smear some on the couple heels of bread that were left in the breadbox. We were arguing over who was the best baseball player. To me, Mickey Mantle was the best, but it was 1961, and Roger Maris had hit sixty-one home runs. That was kind of cool—sixty-one in sixty-one. But I hated the fact that he had broken Babe Ruth's long-standing record of sixty.

"Mickey only had fifty-four homers, but he batted over three hundred," I said.

The screen door closed with a slam. "That's about how many chances that dog has had," Dad said from behind me.

Ronny stood up and backed away from the table. He leaned against the wall with his head down, looking at the floor.

Dad came around and sat down across from me. "That old dog is sucking eggs again, boy," he said in a soft, gentle voice—a voice I had heard only once before when he found out his daddy died. He choked, swallowed, and continued, "To my surprise, Mildred turned out to be a really good dog. She's gotten old now, Tommy. She can barely see or hear anymore. She's not even a good yard dog. She's forgotten that she's supposed to bark when a stranger comes to the house. She has trouble walking, much less chasing any wild animals away. I have more trouble with her than I do with the coons and possums." Dad got up and walked over to the small kitchen closet where we kept the mop, brooms, and a twenty-two single-shot rifle. "It's time now, Tommy, to put her out of her misery."

I jumped up and ran outside, calling for Mildred. She slowly came out from under the porch. She wagged her tail close to the ground, her head down. She had to be wondering why I was screaming at her.

"Down, Mildred. Play dead!" I yelled, as she rolled over on her side. I dropped to my knees, straddling her, and laid my head on her neck.

My tears were flowing freely by then, as one of Mom's Bible stories came into my mind, the one where Jesus was sitting on a mountain overlooking Jerusalem and crying. He had been asking the people to be obedient and repent, or he would have to destroy them.

I hovered over Mildred with my arms spread, my fingers dug into the sand. The tears and mucus mixed together as they ran over my lips. The words from the book of Matthew changed a little as I whispered in her ear. "Oh Mildred, Mildred, how often I have wanted to take you under my wings as a hen does her chicks, but you would not let me."

Dad came out. "You get up from there now, Tommy."

My stomach was hurting like it did when I felt sorry for Ronny. I was sobbing but able to catch my breath just enough to plead with my dad one last time. "Daddy, please don't you shoot my old dog."

I heard the action of the bolt being pulled back and the undeniable sound of a bullet being pushed into the chamber.

"It's over now, Tommy. Get up from there and go inside."

The forward glide and down click of the bolt handle gave me that heavy feeling in my heart, but my brain became clear and full of thoughts. Mildred didn't understand or need repentance. We didn't shoot Grandpa or Grandma when they got sick.

I needed help. "Ronny, Ronny!" I cried. I ran into the kitchen. He wasn't leaning against the wall anymore. I was praying out loud the whole time. "Oh, dear Lord, don't let me hear a gunshot."

I took off down the hallway, turned full speed into the bedroom, and slipped on one of Ronny's papers. I ended up sliding on my butt, stopping halfway into the open closet. Looking up from my backside, I could see that Ronny's clothes were gone. I rolled over to get up and saw that his duffle bag was no longer under the bed.

Thoughts and questions ran through my mind like the newsreel clips at the theater. What if I did hear the shot? Did I want it to be "right on the money," just like the saying, so Mildred didn't suffer. Did I want her to only be wounded, so that during a reload, Dad might change his mind when he saw her suffering? I sat down on Ronny's bed, a broken spirit with that empty feeling of nowhere to turn.

I had my hands over my ears, not wanting to hear the shot. More than that, I couldn't bear to hear a yelping cry from Mildred. What I did hear was Mom's footsteps coming down the hallway. She came into the room and picked up Ronny's paper. She gently pulled off its torn corner where it used to be stapled. She looked down at a couple of Ronny's mismatched socks. He must have dropped them as well on his way out.

"Where's your brother?"

"He's gone, Mom. He's gone."

She sat down on the end of the bed and put her arm around me. "Everything's going to be okay, Tommy. Heavenly Father will make it okay."

I started crying uncontrollably. It had been a long time since I had laid my head in my mother's lap. Her damp dress, with its smell of dish soap, was still soothing to me. She brushed my hair back with her trembling fingers and started reading the piece of paper.

"Remember, Mom, I didn't give that to you. You found it on the floor. Ronny will kill me if you say I gave that to you. Above all, please don't show it to Dad."

Mom stopped reading after the first line and started singing with what Grandma would have described as a "snappy tune."

Mildred and Herman were lovers
Mildred had short scraggly hair
Herman was just another boy on the block
You'd think he was kind of a square
Mildred and Herman been together for years
But little did Herman know
That every time he would fall asleep
Out the door old Mildred would go
She'd fluff up her hair . . .

Mom couldn't finish the song. "That's very cute and very clever," she said, her voice sad.

When she stood up, I saw my name at the top of a note on the back of the paper. "Mom, what does that say on the back?"

She turned the paper over and read the note, her lips moving but making no sound. "You'll have to read that yourself, Tommy," she said, as she laid the paper on the bed. She walked out with her apron pulled up, cradling her face with both hands.

I could hear Mom crying from her bedroom. Between her sobs, she would ask the Lord, and sometimes God, to tell her what she had done wrong. She didn't have to ask God. I knew the answer. She had done absolutely nothing wrong.

I managed to figure out what the note said.

Tommy, practice your reading. Use Bobby's dic. And look it up when you don't know the word. We played a lot of fun games together. So long!

P.S. This is not a game of Catch Me If You Can.

I guess Mom forgot to tell Ronny about abbreviations. I put the paper back in his King Edward private writings cigar box. I hadn't seen that box for years. He always kept it hidden somewhere. He had written *Ronald* in front of *King* and put *Brooks* after *Edward*, because Edward was his middle name. That's why he gave me the TOPS Perfectos cigar box for my marbles. He said it was because I needed to learn Spanish, since English wasn't working out for me that well.

A year had gone by without a word from Ronny. After he left, he never showed up for his job or for his National Guard meetings. Even Ronny's "drugstore cowboy friends" hadn't heard from him. Mom said Dad had all his connections in Cincy keeping an eye out for him in case he showed up there. Dad told me not to bring up his name because it made Mom sad.

Mom had just hung up the phone when I walked in the house. I always tried joking with her, keeping things light as much as she would let me. "Who was that you were talking to?" I asked.

"It was a wrong number," she answered.

"Mom, do you have a secret lover?"

"No, you silly thing. You better not let your father hear you say that. You know how jealous he is."

"Well, if you do, Dad needs to know."

"It was the operator wanting to know if I would accept a collect call from a Johnny Ray Hickenboch. I don't know any Johnny Rays. Do you?"

"No real ones," I said. I sat down at the table trying to hide my happiness.

"Tommy, why are you beaming?" she asked. "Why are you smiling so big? That's the truth, it really was the name of the person calling."

"Is that lemonade in that pitcher?" I asked.

"It sure is. Would you like some? I made it from the lemons off the Davises' tree next door."

"I sure would."

I sipped slowly, trying to think of what to say. Dad didn't know, but I never had to mention Ronny's name. Mom was always asking me if I'd heard anything. She tried not to talk about him in front of Dad because she didn't want to make him feel bad.

"You tell me right now why you're acting so gay. I've never seen your eyes so bright. You've heard from Ronny, haven't you?"

"Yes, well, not directly, but I know he's okay. I know he just wanted to hear your voice."

"Who told you that?"

"Ah . . . one of the National Guards told me. I guess Ronny called them long distance to like, check in."

"Thank ya, dear Lord," she said excitedly. "Thank ya, Jesus! What's the guard's name?"

"He's one of the older guys. I don't know his name. They've all left this morning for two weeks' training."

Mom had hope, and I was hoping Ronny would call back within that next two weeks. Another one of Mom's sayings was that there is "no such thing as a little white lie." I hoped my National Guard lie was allowed to be the first. Indirectly, I did hear from Ronny. I knew he was okay, or at least knew he was still alive. I knew he called just to hear Mom's voice. Maybe God counted it as only a half lie.

In the Bible, Sarah got away with telling a half-truth. Mom told me Sara was Abraham's sister and wife. They had the same dad but different mothers and still got married. Boy, that sure was "way out there." Mom said Sarah was really "choice," and that some jealous guy might kill Abraham to be with her. Abraham asked Sarah to only tell the Egyptian guys that she was his sister so they wouldn't hurt him. I guessed that I had told a half-truth and a half-lie so as not to hurt Mom. The Bible said that God still loved Abraham, so maybe he still loved me.

Being sixteen and in the ninth grade was tough enough. Getting sick to my stomach over math was even worse. My history teacher was sharp. He knew that I knew the material and let me take oral exams instead of written ones. He taught by acting. When the lesson was on George Washington, he dressed like George Washington. He kept my attention as he stood by a little fake cherry tree. When he quoted, "I only regret that I have but one life to give for my country," he acted it out. He explained the Revolutionary War from the eyes of the hanged Nathan Hale by putting on a Confederate officer's hat, pasting the words *Continental soldier* on it, and holding a noose around his neck. I did much better with visual aids, and that was my first and only *B* in high school besides physical education.

It happened. The last day of my sophomore year we moved to that little farm in Pedro. Mom gave our new number to the new owners and to everyone in the neighborhood in case Ronny came back, and once again we waved goodbye. During that summer we built the farm up to ten Black Angus heifers, some fifty chickens, and a dozen smelly pigs.

My grades were just barely good enough to play ball for Lake Weir High. I made the football team and did pretty well for a little guy. I loved game day because we got to wear our jerseys to school. Part of our outfit was a pair of khaki pants with nice starched creases. Mom had gotten up early one Friday morning to iron my pants. She brought them into my room, handed them to me, and said, "Here ya go." She had managed to get three creases down the pant leg when all I desired was one.

I rolled the pants up into a ball and threw them over in the corner. "You mean there they go!" I yelled. "I wouldn't wear those pants to a dogfight."

Usually by that time in the morning Dad was already gone to work. As I heard his footsteps coming down the hallway, I knew I was in trouble. He came into the room and instead of swinging, he said, "Tommy, I want you to go out and slop the pigs. Stay there and watch them eat. Do not take your eyes off of them until I get down there. Do you understand me?"

"Yes, sir, I understand."

I went out and pulled the slop bucket up. We kept it down in the ground so the animals couldn't knock it over. I had the slopping routine down—I had done it every day that whole summer. The bucket was always heavy, but it was extra heavy that morning. The flap lid hadn't closed all the way, and some rainwater had gotten in. It was full of table scraps, stuff like stinky broccoli, leftover runny mashed potatoes, and gravy mixed with soggy bread.

I was able to lug it without stopping all the way to the food bin behind the chicken pen. I scooped a few handfuls of chicken meal into the slop, pushed my sleeve up over my shoulder as always, and reached down into the bottom of the bucket. I grabbed hold of a watermelon rind and a corn cob and stirred in the meal. The ground-up cornmeal made it thicker so the pigs could eat the slop instead of slurping it. As usual I gripped my mixing arm with my other hand. I put my thumb in my armpit, with my fingers across the shoulder. I ran it down the arm, pushing and squeezing off the stuck-on slop.

My next stop, twenty yards away, was the cows' watering trough. Like many times before, I held my breath, stuck my arm in, and rinsed it off. The egg smell from the sulfur well was worse than the slop.

I finally made it to the pigpen, holding the bucket with both hands between my legs. With the help of my knee, I somehow managed to get the bucket on top of the fence. I slowly poured the slop into the *V*-shaped trough. As always, the pigs started in before I could finish pouring. The slop would land on their heads, but once they started eating they didn't stop. Hence the name *pigs,* I presumed.

I stood there as ordered, watching the pigs eat. I had braced my foot against the bottom board of the fence, anxiously awaiting the sure-to-be-open-handed slap to the back of my head. What a dichotomy. I didn't want to get hit, yet I needed to, so I could get to school. If I was eighteen minutes late on game day, I didn't get to play. I never found out why they didn't round it off to twenty minutes.

I continued watching the pigs. It seemed like forever before Dad finally walked up behind me.

"Tommy, have those pigs looked up at you?"

"No, sir."

"You mean to tell me that you've been down here all this time, and they haven't looked up?"

"No, sir, they never look up."

"Tommy, doesn't it amaze you? All the times you've fed these pigs, not once have they ever looked up to see where their blessings come from. Tommy, are you really that dumb? Are you really no smarter than the swine on the other side of this fence? You know that lady in there that you talked to like that, your mother, my wife. Have you no clue as to the many blessings you've received through her?"

I didn't have time to think up any excuses, even if I had wanted to.

"Today I want you to think of her out here on this farm alone. Picture her washing your clothes, changing your bed, and cleaning your room. Among her other chores she will, of course, stop and fix your ever-so-needed pre-game meal. Go on up to the house now and get ready for school."

I made it halfway back to the house when I heard Dad speak again.

"Oh, by the way . . ."

I hated those "oh, by the ways" because I knew a punishment or restriction was coming.

"If I ever hear you talk to your mother that way again, you won't have to worry about wearing those pants to a dogfight, because you won't be able to walk. And that is another blessing from your mother—the only reason you're walking now is that I promised her I wouldn't touch you."

That was a bad morning. I couldn't stop thinking of Mom and all the things she did for me and others. I hadn't ever really thought about it before. I guess I just expected her to do what she did, or maybe I felt it was her job. By lunchtime I had to call her. I went into the secretary's office, turned her desk phone around, and started dialing.

"What are you doing?" the secretary asked. "You're not allowed to use that phone."

"Please, it's an emergency," I said.

"Are you sick?" she asked.

"No, but I will be if I don't talk to my mom," I said.

As soon as Mom picked up the phone I started talking. "I really didn't mean to. I mean, I shouldn't have . . ."

"Tommy, I know. Now you get home as soon after school as you can. You need time for your special supper to digest before playing."

Hard to believe that two of my biggest lessons in life, I

learned from chickens and pigs.

<center>~~~~</center>

I gave up after the eleventh grade. I wouldn't be allowed to play ball that following year because of my age. My friends were all off to school somewhere or in the service. I ended up barely getting my GED on the first try, but I did get it. I wasn't able to enroll in day college but was able to attend night classes at a small junior college. I would find out what instructors taught and tested from their outlined material given in class. If they were teachers who tested from the book with minimal class discussions, I was in trouble. Always sitting in the front row helped me not to daydream. I would reduce the information onto three-by-five cards, keep them in my pocket, and try to memorize them every chance I got.

I managed to get accepted into a university on a probationary status. That meant I had to keep a *C* average and not flunk any class for the first semester. Students on probation had to audit a mandatory college remedial reading class. The word *remedial* alone made me nervous, but not the first word out of the professor's mouth. I was ten minutes late when I walked in.

"Dyslexia may be a nerve problem where the brain has trouble decoding the words," the professor said. "It's not that a dyslexic has trouble reading because he's slow or stupid. It may be due to a biological problem transferring the letters from the eyes to the brain. More studies need to be done. We still don't know for sure if this is the real reason. There's a chance that one of you in this class may even be dyslexic, also known as being 'backward.'"

That was it. That word changed my life, and I had no idea how to spell it. It was the answer to all those years of asking why. A self-diagnosis perhaps, but to me it was a revelation. I sat in that class not hearing another word. All that was going through my mind was, *So I wasn't just slow, dumb, or stupid for all these years.* Well, maybe I was, but that day I became armed with a physiological, biological reason. Vindication, if I wanted to call it that, but justification was enough.

I had an immediate interbody experience. I felt my chest relax and started breathing easier. My heartbeat slowed, my throat loosened, and my head cleared. I felt the heat leave my usually embarrassing red-hot ears. I didn't receive an understanding about "why me?" Instead, my mind gave me the flippant answer of "why not me?" It wouldn't be until later, looking back on my life, that I would realize my indebtedness to dyslexia.

Unknowingly it was dyslexia that made me wonder why. I had to observe, listen, search, and ask. It had given me a whole different outlook on life. One might think that from my view, life would have been short and shallow. To the contrary, it was deep and panoramic. I couldn't only read about the different parts in the game of life. If I wanted to learn them, I usually had to play them.

Ten years had passed since Ronny, alias Johnny Ray Hickenboch, had called. Mom was sick and had gone into the hospital for gallbladder surgery. The doctor opened her up and found that cancer had spread throughout her abdomen. The surgeon sewed her back up and released her to die at home.

A couple weeks passed by. She had gotten so weak that she could barely sit up in bed. As I entered her bedroom one evening, the phone on her nightstand rang.

I picked it up. "Hello," I said.

There was a deep, older, and very caring voice on the other end. "Hi, I'm calling from Nashville, Tennessee. May I please speak to Tommy Brooks?"

"This is he," I replied.

"Do you have a brother by the name of Ronny?" he asked.

"Yes, I do."

"Has anyone called to let you know?"

"Know what?" I asked.

"Son, I regret to inform you." The caller cleared his throat. "Earlier today he was killed crossing a street here in Nashville by a hit and run."

"Are you sure?" I muttered.

"Yes, I was first on the scene. I'm sorry, but he actually passed away in my arms."

The voice paused, and I couldn't speak.

"Would you like to take my name and number down and call me back at a later date? There are things your brother made me promise to tell you."

"No." I didn't dare try to talk, or Mom would know something was wrong.

The older, mature voice continued, "He had this small, stapled pad of songs clutched in his hand that he asked me to send to you. Your name and number are written across the top. I called that number, and they gave me this one. I'm sure the authorities are trying to get in touch with you. I'll make sure they get your new number. Are you still there? Are you okay?"

"Yes."

"Would you like me to continue?"

"Please."

"He said you could share his songs with your mom. Do not show them to your dad unless he asks, but don't hold your breath until he does. He said, 'Tell Tommy to sing my songs. They're stories, bits and pieces of our life together.' Now, let me make sure I get this right." He swallowed and sighed lightly. "Your brother said he was going to see Mildred, that sweet old egg-sucking dog.' Was that his dog?"

"Yes, she was everybody's dog. Is that all, sir? Is that all he said?"

"I think that's about it."

No sooner had I hung the phone up and pulled a chair over close to the bed, but the phone rang again. The voice of the gentleman who had just given me the worst news of my life was calling me by name.

"Tommy, there was one other thing. I was going to let it go, but it's not mine to leave unsaid."

"Please, sir, no matter what it is."

"Your brother was in bad shape, and I tried to keep him from laughing. But as he was saying, 'Mildred, that sweet old egg-sucking dog,' he started smiling and laughing. His last words were, 'Tommy knows that I would never have . . .' He didn't get to finish the sentence."

"He laughed, did you say?"

"Yes, he laughed."

"Would you describe his laugh as just a big smile with him choking back his air?"

"Oh no, I'm sure you're familiar with his laugh. It was the sweetest, most sincere laughter I've ever heard . . . Tommy?"

"Yes, I'm still here."

"You probably haven't heard a lot of sayings in your young life. But if anyone 'died laughing,' it was your brother."

After that awakening conversation I went back over, sat down, and held Mom's hand. I sat thinking how sad for a mother to have never experienced the true laughter of her child.

"Tommy, was that Ronny?"

"That was the last person to talk to him," I said.

"What did he say?"

"He said that Ronny said he was going home."

"Is he flying or driving?"

"I'm sure he's flying, Mom."

"Then I'll get to see him real soon?"

"Yeah, Mom, you're going to get to see him real soon."

I remember becoming deep in thought, stunned over the announcement of Ronny's death. *What do I do? Do I cry? Should I scream, get up and run?* No, I sat there in a stupor as Mom's once nervous little hand turned cold and still. I couldn't let go. In those few dark moments both Ronny and Mom were gone. I became unstable and confused. Sure I was too old for stories, but what if I forgot one or needed a refresher course on love? What if I needed a reminder to be obedient, to tell the truth, or to be kind to others? Who knew more about a broken heart that I could ask other than Mom?

I sat remembering back to the late fifties and being in the parking lot of the first new Sanford Winn-Dixie. Dad and I were sitting in the car waiting for Ronny. He came out pushing, running, and riding on the cart, using it for only one small bag of groceries. He pulled the bag out and jumped in the truck.

Dad reached around me and popped him in the back of the head. "You're not going to leave that basket in the middle of the parking lot, are you?" he asked.

Ronny got out and slowly pushed the cart back toward the front of the store.

"Why does Ronny have to push it back?" I asked.

"Because he has a nonverbal agreement with the owner."

"What's the agreement?"

"The owner agrees to let him use the basket, and he agrees to bring it back."

"Does Ronny know about the agreement?"

"Apparently not."

"Can Ronny and I go over to the Pig and Whistle? We'll just walk home afterwards. Ronny says it's really Smokin'. You can play the jukebox without leaving the booth."

"Be home by dinnertime."

I took off and met Ronny before he was halfway back from his grocery basket return. "Come on, Dad said you can show me the magic jukebox. You don't want to ride home with him anyway."

"Why not?"

"He's mad because you broke your agreement with the owner of Winn-Dixie."

"What agreement? What are you talking about? I don't know the owner. I've never talked to him."

"No, Dad said you have a nonverbal agreement with him about returning his basket."

"Well," Ronny said, "I don't have a verbal or a written agreement, so how am I supposed to know we agreed on a nonverbal agreement?"

"That's exactly what I wanted to know. That's got to be one of Dad's hardest sayings to understand, don't ya think?"

"Don't bother thinking about it."

But there I sat holding Mom's hand and thinking about it. I started wondering if I might have broken any nonverbal agreements with her. I was sure I had, but I couldn't think of any. If she could have, she would have told me "not to worry about such silly things." So I didn't. I did worry about forgetting the things I would have never learned in school— that is, the things I learned from an uneducated mother.

~~~

My dad died a few months later of what I'm sure was a broken heart. He was found dead sitting in the back pew of a church. He was holding a piece of paper on which he had written, *Where did I come from, why am I here, and where am I going?*

Before you say hell, remember we saw the man he was, but we never saw the man he may have strived to be or wished to be. Dad's teaching methods were more direct, with the hands-on approach. If you don't behave, expect a whipping. Be the first to give up the bus seat to the elderly. If not, be ready for a kick in yours. Make sure you recognize the older person in the room first, or you'll recognize something else. Take your hat off when you talk to ladies or expect it to be knocked off. If you lose, figure out why till you win. Don't cry too long about it, or he'll give you something to cry about.

I'm sorry I didn't share all the stories of Dad's many attributes. He did teach me to look a man in the eye when I shook his hand. And that my word should be my bond. He taught me, although not knowingly, that he believed there was one much more powerful than he. I knew he loved me because he never quit reminding me to obey the stop signs.

I did receive Ronny's songs from that nice man and still read them often. Of course, I'm able to read into them and remember the smells, tastes, times, and places. I do sense some anger "interdigitated," if you will, within his lyrics to love and be loved. I had his "Mildred and Herman Were Lovers" song with his goodbye note on the back. I believe that was his first song written at about the age of twelve. He had also left the one with the crazy made-up words about my fifth-grade fight with Billy. I just couldn't see Ronny upgrading or deviating from his homemade notebook. Maybe there's a Nashville pad of songs somewhere. It appears that he only wrote a few songs after our first school bus ride. That was when he became Johnny Ray, and the
~~~

little blond girl "urp slopped" him.

It wasn't that the rhymes or lyrics to Ronny's songs were great, although I do think a few of them are pretty good. It's the irony of all those years of growing up. I thought I had the market cornered on learning by watching, listening, asking, and copying others. Not only was Ronny doing the same, but he was also reading and writing it down. He was actually journaling through his songs. Was I just a little naïve, or did I once again realize "just how dumb is stupid"?

When reminiscing about the past, the somewhat trite but still true sayings of my mom come to mind. When I think of Ronny, who he was and what he might have wished to be, three sayings still haunt me.

"What if" Dad hadn't been so afraid of how we might turn out? What if he hadn't been worrying, living in fear, so affected and influenced by his police work? What if he had stepped back and tried to understand and accept Ronny's laugh and speech.

What if Dad could have instilled the "as if" principle? Ronny might have practiced his speech as if he could have become the next great orator, like Demosthenes. I'm sure he would have used marbles instead of rocks in his mouth to help form his tongue. Just maybe Ronny could have lived as if he were a free agent with freedom to choose. What if, when Ronny showed his effeminate side of love for the arts, dancing and music, Dad could have acted instead of reacted. Ronny just might have gained the self-confidence to live as if he was going to sing like Sinatra and dance like Fred Astaire. What if Dad had taken the time and asked to see what he was writing. Given even the least bit of approval, Ronny might have tried writing songs as if he had a chance to become an Irving Berlin. What if Ronny had been the first or last child instead of the middle? What if . . .

"If only" I had been smarter and braver. If only I could have been able to read Ronny's songs to Mom and Dad. If only I would have made them recognize Ronny's potential. If only I had made Ronny read his songs to me, and I had told him they were great. If only I could have been the older one and taught him how to relax when he talked. If only I would have had a guitar to give him. Just think, if only Dad knew at thirty what he had learned by sixty. If only . . .

I wonder if Ronny ever pitched even one of his songs or ever put them to music. I want to think that he did and that he at least got to say, "Almost."

I should let you know that Dad didn't shoot Mildred, but she did have to go. Apparently, when she would walk with us to the bus stop, she would stay and spend the morning at the store. The owners loved her, and she loved them. For some reason she didn't care for the eggs once they were cleaned and in the basket. She lived another whole year after Ronny had left home. She received a pat on the head and a "Hello, Mildred" from every customer. She was allowed to die of old age, wagging her tail, lying at the door of the Corner Store.

Oh, by the way, I ended up owning the store. I put in new gas pumps, and instead of being a manager, I hired one. Mom and Dad would have been proud. I got married and bragged about having a little boy by giving out cigars. I talked him into naming his first little dog Mildred. I'll let you guess what his name is.

Catch Me If You Can

Verse
I'm drinkin' Monday-morning coffee on Wednesday
    afternoon
Smokin' last week's cigarettes that belonged to you
And I'm sippin' on a cup with lipstick on the rim
Prayin' you're only playin' the game of catch me if you can

Bridge
I've got a clothesline full of laundry that should be taken
    down
And I'm sleepin' on the same sheets that were on when you
    left town
Lookin' at a scrapbook of what we've done and where we've
    been
And prayin' you're only playin' the game of catch me if you
    can

Chorus
Tiddlywinks and pick-up sticks were games we used to play
Spin the bottle and blind man's bluff are games of yesterday
I put away these childish things, since I became a man
But I'm prayin' you're only playin' the game of catch me if
    you can

Verse
I can brew a fresh cup of coffee, change my brand of
    cigarettes
Wash away the color on the cup where your lips pressed
Take down all the laundry, change the linens on the bed
But I'll keep prayin' you're only playin' the game of catch
    me if you can

The Old Sanford Grammar School

About the author

Tom Brooks is a first time author but he had the advantage of being a member of the country club. That is a club member of the fifteen percent of the country who are dyslexic.

He may not be a fully compensated dyslexic but enough to have earned a masters degree in physical education. He claims that for one year he became the absolute worse junior high school teacher and coach of all times. Becoming a physical therapist became his quest. He earned a Bachelor of Science degree in physical therapy by incorporating the "as if," principle. He practiced reading as if he could and he did. He's been a physical therapist and athletic trainer in the private practice setting for forty years in Las Vegas, Nevada.

Tom and his wife Pam have been married thirty five years and have two children, Parker and Casie. And, there's Howard, the English Bull Dog.

Tom also has a son and daughter from a previous marriage, Jason and Ashley. They all hope you enjoy the read.